# SHATTERED ORNAMENTS

## A Holiday Horror Tale

By

Brad Carr

# ABOUT THE AUTHOR

Brad Carr is the creator of the science fantasy novel series, "Enigmas & Empires." His writings are known for their mysterious twists, and controversial topics. He lives in a small country town in Delaware, with his wife Lizzie, and their son Lucas.

# Chapter One

"Bert, the guests will be arriving soon," the butler spoke with a friendly tone.

The gentleman of advanced age, was startled, nearly jumping out of his chair from the sound of the butler's voice. "Oh! Simmons, you scared me. I must've dosed off."

"My apologies Bert, I didn't realize you were sleeping."

"Quite all right, I should have been awake for our guests. Are all the preparations in order?"

"Yes, of course, do you need help getting up?"

"No, I'm fine," Bert replied grabbing a black aluminum cane, next to his maroon high back, leather chair.

His knee caps let out a small cracking noise as he stood. Hunching over, he slowly straightened his back upright, until the muscles loosened enough to move. Bert was a chubby old man, wearing a festive Santa suit of red and white. He combed his swollen fingers through his thinly soft, white hair, and scratched his goatee.

Copious amounts of hardcover books ascended the tall ceiling of his study. Rolling ladders rested on metal tracks, attached to the floor and bookcase. The shelving covered most of the reddish brown, wood grained walls. Copper ceiling tiles reflected the images below. Logs crackled from the flames in the stone fireplace. Above that fireplace, a gold framed painting hung against the wall. The brightly colored landscape, portrayed a similar style of "Monet's Water Lilies," giving light to the otherwise darker tones of the study's atmosphere.

Bert's black boots tapped, while strolling across the dark hardwood floors. Mounted on a wall, he passed by a small display frame. Inside the glass, was a Purple Heart Medal, set against a black felt background. Above it, a five by seven inch frame, matching the display, with a square black and white photograph, of United States Army soldiers.

Bert walked into the kitchen. Next to a matching stove, a silver refrigerator was situated close by, separated from a twenty-eight inch section of counter space. Porcelain mosaic tiles, with varieties of yellow, and brown hues, graced the walls. Lightly stained cherry cabinets stretched across the corner of the kitchen, reaching a side exit door, and halting at the refrigerator.

Bert peeked into the electric stove's window, to view a delicious turkey. He was anxiously anticipating to devour the buttered, and basted bird. Pies of all sorts steamed on the red marble countertops. Gingerbread men, with red gumdrop buttons, and white frosting outlines, sprawled out onto a cookie plate. Bert took an extended whiff of the aroma emanating from the counter. The sweet smell of apple pie made his mouth water. Bert thought to himself, "One little nibble of crust from the edge couldn't hurt." But just about the time he was going to peel off a sliver, Simmons interrupted him.

"Bert! Not yet, we have to wait for the guests."

"Wait, don't I pay you? Didn't I purchase the groceries?"

Simmons sighed, "Yes you did. But I was instructed by you to prevent any eating before Christmas dinner."

"I said that?"

"Yes."

"Damn, okay. Guess I'll wait. What about the honey glazed ham? Can I have a piece of that?"

"Patience."

"Fine. Guess I'll just starve."

"Don't be overdramatic."

Bert laughed in a high pitch, with an uncontrolled wheeze, and replied, "That's what I like about you Simmons, you keep me straight."

"Bert, why don't you wait in the den? I'll bring the guests in, while you rest in your favorite chair."

"I don't want to rest. Hey! I got it! I'll put on some festive music. Should I get the record player from the bedroom?"

"It would be easier to use the satellite radio."

"We have that? I didn't realize I spend so much money on frivolous things."

"Yes, you do sometimes. But I'll take care of turning it on for you."

"Okay, but I like the nostalgia of record players. When you have records, you treat them with care. Like a delicate vase. People don't treat things with care anymore, do they Simmons? But I concede, I'll just greet the guests."

"Whatever you wish. Oh, I forgot, I put egg nog on a serving table in the den for the guests. Would you like me to serve you a glass?"

"I'm perfectly capable of taking care of it. Wait, I just realized. Where is the kitchen staff tonight?"

"They left a few minutes ago to spend the holiday with their families tonight. But they prepared the meals before they left. All I have to do, is set the table, and remove the turkey in an hour."

"I'm so glad. They should spend time with their loved ones on Christmas. I'll wait in the den. Just, let me know if you need me to sample something. You know? To make sure it is up to par with our guests."

"Nice try Bert. Per your instructions, you said…"

"I know what I said," Bert interrupted, yet in a humorous nature. "God Simmons, you really are too serious," he giggled.

Bert had a spring in his step tonight. He was in a warm mood. Christmas was his favorite holiday. Bert seemed to brighten up the day after Thanksgiving, every year. He would begin setting up decorations early. Usually, he received a burst of energy, and a hankering to hang holly wreathes around the house, after an early Thanksgiving dinner. Then, he would settle down, and watch the last football game to be broadcasted. It was his personal tradition.

Beautifully illuminated with clear string lights, a pine tree, decorated in silver bulbs, and gold ribbon trim, sat in the corner of the den. A disfigured angel, created from paper mache, obviously made with a child's hands, was situated on top of the peak. Seven presents were wrapped in brown shipping paper and a twine bow. Bert liked the basic forms of wrapping paper, because it flooded his mind with pleasant Christmas memories with his father.

Glossy white paint covered the walls of the den. Chair railing trim, made of lacquered oak, encircled the perimeter. Winter landscape paintings filled up every wall. Horse-pulled sleds with passengers, carolers serenading in front of cabins, children building snowmen, dogs hopping through the snow, and many more holiday images filled the frames.

Music pushed melodies at a comfortable volume, from the speakers throughout the estate home. "Cool Yule," sung by Louis Armstrong, began its positive beat. Bert began to dance as well as an elderly man could. Small subtle motions of bending his knees, slight head bobbing, he had a confident strut, approaching the serving table. Bert reached the egg nog bowl located behind one of the creme colored sofas. Grabbing a four ounce glass with a tiny handle, he poured it to the brim, with thick egg nog, using a silver ladle. Topping it off with a sprinkle of cinnamon, the spice floated on top.

Taking a sip, his eyes lit up. “Simmons! Needs more rum doesn’t it?”

“There’s plenty in there Bert,” Simmons answered, with a heightened volume from the kitchen, so Bert could hear him. “We don’t need our guests getting drunk off one glass!”

“Oh, fine then, don’t be such a party pooper! I’ll leave it be.” Bert took another sip and murmured, “It does taste, good enough, I guess.”

“I’m putting out another bowl for the kids, one without rum, in just a minute. It’ll be in the rose colored glass punch bowl. Make sure you tell the guests when they arrive.”

“Good point, I will.” Then Bert muttered under his breath again, “I swear, who is the employee, and who is the employer in this house?” Bert traveled into the foyer. Clicking his fingers to the beat of the holiday music, playing throughout every room. “Gotta love Louis Armstrong,” he whispered to himself.

Opening the front door made of sturdy oak, he exited out into the front porch. Warm air steamed from his mouth. The snow delicately floated like feathers on a slight breeze, zig zagging gracefully without a specific pattern. The moonlight reflected off the icy ground. Bert enjoyed the snow, although his arthritic bones didn’t.

The concrete porch was rather small compared to his large house. Most people considered this a mansion, but

Bert always called it a house. A long asphalt lane divided through the landscape on the hill, and descended to the small country road. Holiday lights from other homes, shone bright from nearly a half-mile away.

"Bert what are you doing out here?"

"Jesus! Simmons stop walking up behind me and scaring the living hell out of me!"

"Sorry, but you know what the doctor said, this weather is horrible for your arthritis."

"Simmons I am an old man. Who knows how many more snowfalls I have left? I'll be inside soon."

"Okay Bert. Just do me a favor and don't walk onto the steps. They're slippery, I have to put more salt on them. In fact, I'll do that now. Why don't you go inside and wait for our guests?"

Bert grabbed a hand full of snow from the porch railing. He packed it tightly into a snowball. When Simmons wasn't looking, Bert threw it, hitting him on the back of the head.

"Ha!" Bert exclaimed, then snickered.

"What the…Bert!"

"Oh, you're too serious Simmons. Fine, I'll go in for a while, but you owe me a snowball fight later."

"I'm not going to do that Bert."

"Party pooper."

Bert trekked back to the den. Picking up the glass of egg nog he left behind earlier. He gulped it down. He then proceeded to pour another, and plopped down on a love seat opposite the couch. Impatiently waiting, he began singing under his breath, along to the tune of Burl Ives classic, "Holly Jolly Christmas." The song played ever so crisp, in enhanced quality speakers.

A few minutes later, Simmons entered the den, holding his coat and shoes. He didn't wish to track any snow or salt onto the floor.

"Bert, I am going to get the table settings ready."

Bert nodded. The door bell rang out a few minutes later. But it was a rushed type of ringing. Ding! Ding! Ding! Ding! Ding! Bert was finally able to get to his feet on the fifth ring as it continued. "Hold on! I'm trying to get there as soon as possible!" he called out in an amiable tone.

Shuffling to the brass handle of the front door, he opened it. There on his porch, was a teenage girl, possibly sixteen or seventeen years old, with long blonde hair, and pale skin. Mascara dripped down the crease opening of her eyes. She wore blue jeans, and a button-up top with small pink flower print across a white background. Her arms were crossed, her body shivered from the cold weather.

"Goodness young lady, where is your coat? It's freezing out there."

"I am so sorry to bother you sir, but my van broke down, and I need to use the phone."

"You don't have a cell phone?"

She looked at him with a puzzled look on her face. "A cellphone? Umm, no, I don't own a cell phone?"

"Oh my poor girl, please come in, come in, I insist. You may use my house phone."

Bert stepped back, allowing her a path to entry. She entered, after shuffling her green rubber boots on the textured floor mat outside. “Thank you mister.”

“Bert, my name is Bert.”

The girl held out her cold right hand, and shook his. Introducing herself to him, she stated, “My name is Mary.”

“What happened to your coat?”

“Left the house without one. I forgot it back home. I wasn’t thinking clearly. But I was driving back home, after riding for about twenty minutes. My van broke down near your house.”

“It’s not a problem. Simmons!” Bert called.

Simmons didn’t answer. “Stay here, I will go get the cordless.”

Bert walked to his study, and grabbed the house phone off the wall. Trekking back to Mary, standing in the foyer, he handed it to her. Dialing a number, she then held it to her ear.

“There’s no connection,” she replied. “But it has no cord, so how could it?”

“Because it’s a cordless phone. Haven’t you heard of a cordless phone?”

“Ours phone at home has a cord.”

“Really?” Bert asked in disbelief. Mary returned the phone to him, and he placed it to his ear. No dial tone. “Hold on young lady. I’ll go and fetch my cell phone.” Bert walked back to the den, and picked up his cell phone, that he rested on the serving table. He returned, handing her his large buttoned device.

"What's this?"

"It's my cellphone."

"How's it work?"

"Just dial the number, and press send. Oh, never mind, I'll do it for you," he said with a friendly smile. "What's the number you wish to call?" Mary gave him the number, yet didn't give him an area code. He naturally assumed it was his own area code. Bert dialed and pressed send, holding it to his ear. Nothing happened. Removing it from his right ear, he gazed at the screen. A message read, 'NO SIGNAL.'"Well, darn it. Can't get a tone. Tell you what, why don't you have a seat in the den, and I'll ask Simmons if we can use his phone? Is that okay? At least you'll warm up."

"Thank you."

"Follow me."

***

Simmons exited the bathroom when Bert located him walking out. "Oh good, I found you. We have an unexpected guest."

"An unexpected guest?"

"There's a young lady sitting in the den. Her van broke down, and she wanted to use our phone. But the lines are down, apparently. I gave her my cell phone, but we don't have service. I was wondering, if we could try yours?"

"Yes, of course," Simmons agreed. Pulling out the smartphone from his pocket, he looked at the screen."The towers must be down. I don't have a signal either."

"What do you suggest we do?"

"I'm sure we'll get a signal soon. I'll offer the lady some egg nog from the rose colored bowl, that I sat on the serving table."

"The girl seems like she's had a hard day. Her mascara is running, she must have been crying. Maybe we can invite her to stay, and have dinner with the rest of the guests."

"You want to let a complete stranger stay in your home?"

"She's harmless. Poor girl doesn't even have a coat. Besides, it's Christmas. Good will towards men, and all that. I'll go keep her company, you continue preparations."

"If that's what you prefer, you're the boss."

Bert walked away and entered the den. Mary sat quietly, on the couch, staring ahead, still quivering. Her hands were wedged beneath her arm pits. Pouring her a glass of virgin egg nog, he handed it to her.

"Thank you," Mary said, reaching out to the full glass.

"Apparently none of the phones are working. Telephone lines must be down, we're not getting a signal either. I'm sure it will be up and running soon. You are welcome to stay for Christmas dinner. I have a few guests about to…" Bert's statement was cut short, by the doorbell ring. "Oh, excuse me, I have to answer that."

There was a family waiting outside his entrance when he opened the door. The father of the family was a man wearing a flannel coat over his faded, blue denim overalls, and a straw hat. He appeared to be aged into his mid thirties, with a brown bushy mustache, and black framed spectacles.

"Bert, good to see ya."

"You too Al, please come in."

Two children entered the threshold first. The boy was eight years old, wearing khaki pants, and a green flannel shirt tucked in, behind his belt. Large wet spots covered his brown coat, from playing in the wet snow. His furry Santa hat was too large for his head, but his large ears held it up slightly, below his eyebrows. Healthy in appearance, yet he was small framed. Wisps of light blonde hair, curled out of the rim, of his festive hat.

"Hi, Mister Bert."

"Hello Junior. My you're getting big."

"I'm going to be nine soon, Mister Bert."

"Wow! Congratulations, I wish I could be nine years old again. Oh, don't forget to wipe your feet on the entry rug, please."

A little girl trailed behind him. She was near the same age as Junior, but younger by ten months. Her red curly hair flipped up around her knitted, white rabbit fur cap, covering her little ears from the cold. She wore a green velvet dress, white stockings, and black dress shoes. A black wool peacoat, reached to her knees. The girl wrapped her arms, around Bert's waist, embracing him.

"Hello Mister Bert!" she exclaimed, looking up with her freckled face, and brown eyes. Releasing him she asked, "Do you like my new dress? Papa got it for me!"

"It looks fabulous Hannah," Bert replied with a grin. "You look just like your Mama."

"Hello Bert," the mother greeted him with a kiss on the cheek.

She was younger than her husband, in her late twenties. Her long auburn locks were slicked back into a red ribbon, tying her hair into a bun, near the nape of her slender neck. The mother wore a red and green plaid dress, hiked up just below the knee, with bright red lipstick to match her apparel. A coat of squirrel fur was draped over her clothes. Hooped silver earrings dangled from her lobes.

"Good to see you again Esther. Keeping Al out of trouble?"

"More like keeping her out of trouble," Al snickered.

Esther gave Al an annoyed stare from his comment. Her expression made Bert a little uncomfortable. He knew Al didn't mean any ill will, only a bit of humor, that she clearly didn't enjoy. Quickly changing the subject, Bert asked, "Why don't I take your coats?

Placing their coats on the rack near the door, Junior tugged at the side of Bert's pant leg. "Mister Bert? Is it okay if I play with your train set?"

"I wanna see it too!" Hanna exclaimed.

"It's okay with me if it's okay with your parents. Just don't touch the ones in the display case."

Al gave the kids a nod of approval. Their little faces beamed with excitement. Hannah jumped up and down tapping her shoes on the floor.

"Neat! Is it still in the room next to the study?" Junior asked.

"Yes, I set it up for you yesterday, I knew you would ask. Have fun you two."

"Thanks Mister Bert!"

As the kids wandered off, Bert spoke, "We have some egg nog. Please join me."

Al and Esther followed Bert into the Den. He introduced them to Mary, while pouring their glasses. After a bit of introductory chit-chat, Bert asked Al, "So, how did the crop do this year? I haven't been able to speak with you for a while," Bert stated.

"It was a decent year. We had a small profit, but we got by okay. Much better than the year before."

"We could have done better," Esther joined in, after she gulped down the glass, and poured another in a matter of a minute. "We were hoping to get one of those new Ford Coupes. But Al insisted we keep his old rickety truck."

"I like my truck Esther."

"Yeah, but the kids are getting too big to sit on the bench between us."

Realizing the conversation was about to turn into an argument, Al changed the subject. Directing his conversation to Mary, he asked, "So, Mary is it?"

"Yes," she replied.

"We can give you a ride home if you wish."

"That would be great. Thank you."

"I'll go get the truck warmed up. You don't live too far, right?"

"What about dinner?" Esther asked.

"Oh, we can be back in no time. I'm sure it will only be a few minutes drive down the road."

"I live closeby," Mary confirmed.

"Bert, would it be okay if I leave the kids here, while Esther and I take the young lady home?"

"Not a problem, I would be delighted."

"Why do I have to go?" Esther asked.

"Well, I'm sure Mary wouldn't be comfortable riding in a truck with some man she just met. What would people say? I'm sure she would feel more comfortable if a woman rides along."

"No," Esther coldly stated, while standing near the punch bowl, pouring back another egg nog quickly."

"But Esther, I'm…"

"It's okay, I will stay until you both are ready to leave," Mary intervened, so as to not stir up an expanding argument.

"What about my butler? I can get him to take you home," Bert suggested.

"No, it's fine. I will graciously wait."

"I would be honored if you do. Unless you have to go somewhere for your own Christmas dinner," Bert offered to confirm again.

"No, not tonight I'm afraid. I would be glad to join you for dinner." Mary replied.

"You won't regret it. We have a big turkey, honey glazed ham, pies of all sorts, yams, mashed potatoes, well you get the point. We will have a gigantic surplus of food to spare."

The door bell rang out again. Bert caught a glimpse of Simmons approaching the foyer, from the hallway, to greet the next guest. Entering the den, was a college student from the state university. He wore a blue collegiate jacket, denim jeans, and white shirt. His jet black hair was slicked backward.

"Bert, my man! Good to see ya," he greeted, strutting over to shake his hand.

"Richey, welcome back. I take it you've been hitting the books over your winter break?"

"No way Bert, don't be a square," he replied jokingly.

"Oh, where are my manners?" Pointing to the guests in the room, "Richey this is Al, his wife Esther, Junior and Hannah are running around here somewhere, and this is Mary."

"Pleasure to meet y'all."

"Likewise," Esther said, giving Richey a seductive yearning in her eyes, poking out her chest a little further, to highlight attention to her breast regions.

"We are expecting one more guest," Bert announced."She should be here any minute."

***

Another guest arrived at Bert's front door. He greeted her and said, "Hello Olivia. Good to see you, Merry Christmas."

She was a young woman, in her mid twenties, with shoulder length sandalwood hair, and sullen hazel eyes. Keeping her head turned, she replied, "Thank you. You too Bert."

Bert noticed a slight blue hue under her make up, beneath her left eye. A small, but obvious puffiness, surrounded her cheekbone. "Would you like to come in?"

"Yes," Olivia spoke in hushed, depressed tone.

Bert introduced Olivia to everyone in the room, and offered her a spot on the sofa. He poured a glass of egg nog, and handed it to her. She thanked him. The two children circled through the den at full speed, almost causing Olivia to spill her glass. They raced into the wide open rooms, giggling hysterically.

"Kids! Stop running through Bert's house!" Esther scolded the children.

"Oh, I don't mind if you don't Esther. I'm not worried about anything breaking."

"That's not the point Bert, I don't want them galavanting like savages."

"Sorry Esther, I was just letting you know, I didn't mind on my end, that's all. I wasn't intruding on your parenting style," Bert stated.

"No need to apologize," Al chimed in.

Changing the subject, "Well I guess now that everyone is here, we might as well begin eating. Please, follow me to the dining room." Bert's left hip began to give him pain while directing the guests. He had a noticeable limp, merging to his left side, and slight drop in his walking pattern.

Entering a wide hallway, of dark mahogany wood panels, filled with antique portrait pantings of historical figures, the guests passed the entrance to the study. The next entry to the left side, was the dining room, connected to the kitchen.

Echoes filled the dining room as they entered. An abundance of space filled the room. The table was shaped like a wide rectangle. Eight seats, spaced a foot apart from one another, were pushed under the bright red table cloth. The room was elegantly lit. A gold candelabra with seven arms rested on the middle of the table, tiny flames danced on the wicks. Silver and gold Christmas bulbs, with bottom segments of white, frosted paint, encircled the base of the candelabra. Holly wreathes hung on the perimeters of the walls, spaced five feet apart from one another. String lights covered the high ceilings, emulating the multitudes of stars in the night skies.

Shining white ceramic plates, were placed in front of each chair. Gleaming silverware rested on top of green cloth napkins. Simmons began pouring water from a pitcher into one of the crystal stemmed glasses, for each place setting. Champagne bottles rested inside two ice receptacles. A red punch bowl was provided for the children, and Mary.

Delicious food rested on the median of the long dining table. On a tray, the plump turkey steamed through lightly crisped skin; a carving knife was positioned near the side. Half of the honey glazed ham was sliced an eighth of an inch in thickness, piling up on the silver serving tray. Marshmallow yams, garlic red skinned mashed potatoes, panned fried asparagus, steamed broccoli covered in melted cheddar cheese, caesar salad with croutons, and freshly baked sourdough bread, orchestrated a symphony of aromas, making the guests mouth water.

"Please, everyone be seated."

Simmons carved the turkey, and served everyone their meal. Differing conversations flooded the air between bites over the next forty minutes. Hannah and Junior talked about Santa's arrival. Al spoke of his desire to win the grand prize for the largest hog next year. Richey bragged about his two door sedan with a flathead V8 engine. Esther expressed her desire to visit the beautiful shores of Honolulu. By now the liquor had taken effect, and she was slurring a few words.

Everyone seemed to be enjoying themselves. But there were two exceptions. Mary and Olivia whispered to one another, with serious expressions painted on their faces. Olivia's eyes began to glass over, and her lip began to tremble. It appeared as though Mary was comforting Olivia, by an empathetic touch to her forearm.

Richey was seated beside Esther, listening to Al's enthusiastic stories about the farm. A tiny smirk painted Esther's face. Richey's eyes opened wide with shock. He looked uncomfortable, and distant. Bert realized that Richey became distracted. Pretending to drop his napkin, Bert peaked under the table. Esther was slowly rubbing Richey's crotch through his pants.

Attempting to help Richey out of an uneasy situation, and avoid a dramatic scene, Bert stood up and announced, "How about some pie? Richey why don't you help me bring it to the table.

Simmons protested, "I can handle that."

"No, really it's good to stretch my legs for a moment. Do you mind?"

"Of…of course not. No problem," Richey replied, sliding out his chair from the table, and rising.

Entering the kitchen together, Bert asked, "Richey, what's going on? I looked under the table."

"I swear Bert. I didn't provoke her, I…"

Bert interrupted him, "No I know that. It's no secret that Esther gets a little," he paused, "rowdy when she drinks. Luckily, I don't think Al noticed anything."

"Oh, thank God," Richey sighed with relief. "What do I do?"

"Dinner is almost over anyway, we can…"

Bert's sentence was halted by the screeching yell of Hannah in the dining room. Dashing as rapidly as possible, to the dining table, Bert and Richey witnessed Al consoling the frightened little girl.

"What happened?" Bert asked.

"Oh it's nothing. Hannah thought she saw something in the corner. But it's nothing, just a child's imagination working overtime."

"Daddy, please. I'm not making it up. I saw it. It looked at me! It told me to jump!" she wailed.

"Hush now. Calm down," Al spoke while hugging her. "It's okay."

"Psshh!" Junior joined in, mocking his sister. "I told her that Frankenstein movie would scare her. What a scaredy cat."

"You shut up Junior!" Hannah exclaimed.

"Enough! Both of you!" Al said in a boisterous tone. "No arguing here, it's impolite."

The string of light bulbs exploded in plethora of glass pieces, in the corner of the room, near the window. Half the dining room was covered in darkness. Esther gasped in fright, "Wha….What is that?!"

The moonlight from the window revealed a tall shadow standing in front of it. Calm was sucked out of the room, and replaced by utter chaos. Everyone except for Bert, and Al, remained behind while the panicked guests retreated.

Boldly, Al stood in front of Bert. "Who are you? Leave this house immediately!"

Stepping partially into the illuminated area was Simmons. However, his complexion seemed odd. All blood flow, in his face diminished. He was as pale as a corpse. Simmons stepped closer, dragging his feet slowly, with his neck dangling, like plumb bob in a gusty wind storm. Black glossy eyes looked up at Bert, with a tilted head positioned off center.

"Simmons, this isn't funny. Stop scaring everyone!"

In a deep guttural voice, Simmons replied, "They should be frightened."

Gulping in fear, Bert replied in a cracking voice, "What do you want?"

"I've come to consume life."

"Stay away!" exclaimed Al, grabbing the carving knife from the turkey tray.

Simmons widely opened his mouth. Purple veins protruded from his face, and traveled up his neck. Slivering out, his tongue curled outward like a serpent, split into elongated forked ends. Lips stretched out, ripping tears around long, jagged teeth, connecting to his extended jawline.

Al grabbed Bert by the right arm. "Run Bert!"

But Bert couldn't move. His legs stiffened like concrete in a desert heat. Al escaped, leaving Bert behind.

"Oh Bert, you are all alone now. Some man Al turned out to be huh? Leaving a defenseless boy like you behind."

"B…boy?"

Simmons leapt up five feet in height, angling forward, landing on top of the table. Pulling the table cloth around his talon feed, food crashed to the floor. Stretching out long claws from his pink fleshy fingertips, his neck extended downward. Simmons' unholy profile halted just an inch from Bert's face. Bert compressed his eyelids, trying to avoid Simmons' image. He waited for his life to end.

# Chapter Two

Bert held in his breath. Seconds passed by, which seemed like minutes to Bert's frightened state. Yet, nothing happened. Opening his eyelids, starting with the left, he appeared to be alone in the dining room. Simmons was missing. Void of any food, the table was spotless and untouched. Plates and utensils were glimmering from the reflections of the lights above, resting on the table top surface. Chairs were put back under the table, as if no one had attempted to sit. Oddly, the table cloth, was green. Just a few moments ago, it was red. The Christmas lights that shattered earlier, on the on the farthest side of the room, were unbroken.

"Bert, it's not time for dinner yet," Simmons stated, startling him to where his body jerked.

"Simmons?"

"Yes, who else would I be?"

"But your face, it's normal again. What happened to you?"

"What in the world are you talking about Bert?" Simmons questioned in a perplexed and worried tone.

"I guess, I had a bad dream."

"Did you fall asleep on the floor again?"

"No, no nothing like that, just a daydream, I guess."

"Hmm, well the rest of the guests should be arriving soon."

"Rest of the guests? Aren't they here already?"

"Al and his family aren't here yet."

"But, they arrived over an hour ago."

"Bert, are you sure you're okay? The only guests who've arrived so far are Olivia, Richey, and that stranded girl. What was her name again? Right, Mary was her name. Completely slipped my mind. Anyhow, why don't you keep the guests entertained?"

Bert began to question his own sanity. Yet, he accepted the strange events he witnessed, as inconsequential as a daydream, or the imaginations of an aging mind. Maybe he fell asleep with a horror movie on the television, and it crept into his brain for a later date. "You're right Simmons. I'll get to it then."

"Very good, I have to finish some preparations. I'll get the door when Al arrives."

"No, it's fine Simmons. I'll answer it. I enjoy greeting the guests."

"Okay, they're your guests after all."

Heading back to the den, Bert noticed the decorations were placed into different positions. The sofa and love seat were rearranged in opposite places. A present was missing from under the tree, now six presents remained.

"Bert, where have you been? Sneaking a few crumbs from the kitchen?" Richey questioned with a smirk on his face.

Bert's mood lightened and replied, "I tried to, but Simmons wouldn't let me.

"Very funny Bert, ha! Who is Simmons? Kind of an odd first name isn't it? Ironic maybe."

"You know, Simmons, my butler."

"Butler? Man you really are moving up in the world. You have a kitchen staff working tirelessly in there already."

"No, I sent the kitchen staff home for the holiday."

"Then who is in the kitchen, cooking that delicious smelling food? I know you didn't do it. You could burn water," Richey teased, as he sometimes does.

"Excuse me for a second Richey."

Bert exited, and peeked his head into the kitchen. Mrs. Purse was rotund and jolly, wearing her spotless chef uniform of glowing white. She wore a net, over her salt and peppered hair. Mrs. Purse was basting a turkey, with the oven door open. Her assistant Claude, ferociously whipped the mashed potatoes in a bowl. Claude was a skinny man, wearing a sky blue apron, with a few spots of grease on the fabric. His buttoned shirt was long sleeved and black, with gray pinstripe dress pants.

"Did you need anything Mister Bert?" Mrs. Purse asked with husky voice, peering up to him.

"No, I'm fine. Just ah, checking on how the dinner's coming?"

"Shouldn't be too long now."

"Did Simmons or I tell you, that you could return home tonight, to spend time with your families?"

"Yes, Mister Bert, you informed us a week ago. We're going to make sure we set the table before we leave. Is that sufficient?"

"Of course, keep up the good work. Oh, and if I don't see you leave, Merry Christmas. Have a happy New Year too."

"Merry Christmas," Claude and Mrs. Purse replied in unison.

Bert shuffled along the first floor, searching for Simmons. He thought for sure that Richey knew who he was. He's met him before. Yet, as the minutes passed, there wasn't any sign of Simmons' location.

"Maybe he's outside in the garage. I'll check on him later. Would be rude of me to leave the guests for too long," he thought to himself.

*Ding dong!* The door bell rang. Opening the front door, he greeted Al.

"Al, how are you? Merry Christmas!" Bert exclaimed in an excited tone.

Al appeared to be downcast. He kept his head hung low. Gazing up to return the greeting, his eyes appeared tired, irritated, and void of hope. "Hello Bert," he replied in an unusually monotonous tone. "Merry Christmas to you too, we're getting by. Esther and Junior are on their way. She dropped me off, while she went to pick up rum, for the egg nog."

"That's not necessary, we have plenty here. In any case, I always keep a stocked shelf."

"She told me you requested it."

"Did I? Maybe I did and I just don't remember. But please, come in from the cold. How is that prize pig you've been bragging about?" Bert asked, while Al entered the foyer.

"Oh, I'm afraid the hogs are a little frail this year. May I, use your bathroom?"

"Sure, you know where they are. We're meeting in the den when you finish. Richey, Olivia, is here, oh, and an unexpected guest. Poor girl's van broke down. I figured I'd let her stay for dinner until we give her a ride."

"Okay."

Al wasn't his typical, cheery self. Bert couldn't understand why he was so depressed. Al loved the winter holiday. He was so energetic when he spoke about Christmas. His eyes seemed to light up when he spoke about Santa Claus to the kids. Yet, this time, he appeared to be apathetic to the holiday. Clearly, there were burdens, that Al was feeling too exhausted to carry.

***

An hour had trickled away. Esther was extremely late. To ensure the dinner remained warm, Bert decided to allow the guests to eat dinner without her. Entering the dining room, the table was decorated in a similar arrangement as before, with subtle differences. The guests were seated.

Bert approached the kitchen, expecting to see Simmons. But Simmons, was still absent. The kitchen staff had left for the rest of the week. So Bert took it upon himself to carve the turkey. Each guest walked around the table, serving themselves.

Mary and Olivia began conversing, and smiling. This was an opposite reaction, than Bert's daydream revealed earlier in the night. Richey began discussions on the topic of the Cold War. They were all enjoying themselves, except for Al. He spun his food around with his fork, staring intently into the center of the plate.

"It's going to be an all out nuclear holocaust. As soon as I buy a home, I'm going to install a fallout shelter," Richey announced.

"Why would you need that Richey?" asked Bert. "The cold war is ov…."

"Because I want to survive the coming armageddon," Richey interrupted. "Have you seen the footage of the atomic bomb victims of Hiroshima and Nagasaki? That's stuff is scary as hell. I'm going to make sure I build a strong structure. Gotta build a bathroom in there, equipped with a shower, and toilet, and everything. Then I have to make sure I have a hotplate for food, cupboards full of canned goods too. I mean, it could be years until the surface is safe again. We may need entertainment, so I want to make sure I have lots of shelves, full of books too. Hopefully a little woman will be with me, if you catch my drift," he snickered. "Oh, and guns, you gotta have guns. You might have to hunt when your food supplies are low, that is, unless there isn't any life on the planet. But hey, it's better than no chance at all. If those communists have their way, we would all be dead."

"Communists?"

"You know, the Russians."

"Richey, we are at peace with Russia."

"We're never at peace with the USSR"

"What the hell are you talking about Richey? The USSR is no more. It failed."

"Do you got a time machine or something Bert? Can you give me the lottery numbers for the week?"

"The party girl is here!" Esther announced, staggering in the dining room with a half-filled bottle of rum in her hand. "Junior! Get your ass in here, and sit down."

"Yes, Mama," Junior obeyed, entering with a miserable expression.

"See that Al!" She belched while speaking. "It only takes a good little ass whoopin' to get this damned kid straight. If you had whooped him some more, our Hannah might still be alive."

Bert was shocked to hear this. His mouth gaped open as questions swirled inside his mind. 'Hannah is dead? When did this happen? What could have possibly happened to such a sweet little girl? Hannah was just here? Wasn't she? Why can't I remember something as awful as this? And why was it Junior's fault?' Bert struggled to keep these questions to himself. He didn't know, or understand, how to respond, to a tragedy that words cannot comfort.

"Now stop it Esther," Al stood up in defense of his son. "They were just playing as kids do. Don't blame Junior! He's just a boy."

"I'll blame who the hell I feel like. You aren't much of a man Al. I should go ahead and fuck Richey. I could teach that young man, how to stick it in me real good! At least I'll get more than you give me!"

"Woah, woah, woah!" Richey chimed in. "I don't sleep with married women."

"You're drunk Esther," Al confirmed. Turning to Bert, he said, "I think we need to leave Bert. Thank you for a lovely dinner. But my wife, has had too much to drink."

"Mama, I'm sorry. I didn't mean it. I promise." Junior pleaded with tears flowing down his cheeks.

"Shut up you little shit stain!" Esther stomped over to the little boy, reaching her arm back, and slapping him across the face. A red irritation swelled immediately on his right cheek.

"That's enough!" Al approached Esther grabbing her tight across her shoulders, shaking her. "She was my daughter too dammit! But you don't see me covering up her memory with booze! Junior is our son! Bad things happen to good people! We can't blame him!"

Shoving his hands away from her, Esther replied, "Is that what you tell yourself Al? You walk around like a dead man! You don't even notice us anymore! You let our crops go to hell! The farmhouse is a disaster! You haven't touched me in over a year! How dare you! You should have been watching the kids more closely!"

"Stop it Esther. You got to stop," he begged in a quiet voice.

The Christmas lights bursted from the ceiling again, crashing down shards of glass on the hardwood floor. Only the candelabra illuminated the darkness. A penetrating laugh surrounded the room, bouncing an echo off the walls.

Standing near the same window in which Bert remembered the ghastly image of Simmons, was a lanky shadow standing nearly ten feet in height. All of the guests stood in awe, gasping in terror. The muscles in their legs simulated petrified wood. Although they wished to escape, the pure curiosity of human nature, took control over their common sense.

Stepping into the candlelight, the creature revealed its hideous form. Unnaturally bony, elongated arms reached the surface of the floor, bending at the elbows. Stalking forward slowly, cramped pointed knees crawled. Two gangly feet, made up of three misshapen toes, were on each foot. Thumping to a loud rhythm in the guests ears, a necklace of gooey, pumping human hearts, hung from small metal cages, around its skeletal-like neck. The monster's oval shaped head, seemed gigantic compared to its slender body. Enormous egg shaped eyes, with yellow irises, and sclera, gazed directly at Al. Fleshy textures of the creature's skin dripped a crimson, gummy ooze, puddling on the floor.

Pointed teeth stained in a beige, tar crusted hue, revealed a sneer when it spoke in a deep guttural voice, "The reaper took a seed, a man lost his fight. I've come for his heart, on this cold winter's night."

Bing Crosby's "White Christmas" blasted through the house speakers in a thunderous volume. The guests began sprinting, and stumbling over each other to leave. Al picked up Junior, heaving him up over his shoulder, in one continuous swoop, taking flight. A shot of adrenaline gushed through Bert's veins. Although the others were faster than he, and ahead of his pace; terror finally influenced his sense of urgency.

The creature galloped out of the kitchen, clumsily sliding into the wide hallway, hitting the wall, and busting it down. Knocking Bert to the floor, it leapt past him. Arriving swiftly to the front door, before the guests could escape, the monster blocked them in.

"I am the Widow Maker. Halt and you will see. I only need one, and it is he," the Widow Maker pointed to Al with its long crooked fingers.

Al gently put Junior down beside him. He stared at his son. Al's shoulders slumped forward, with an expression of defeat in his mannerisms. Bravely gazing into the Widow Maker face, he agreed, "It's okay. You can take me. Just let the others escape. I am ready."

Pulling back its right arm, the Widow Maker was about to strike. But it was distracted, by a swift blow to the head with Bert's cane. Thunk! The Widow Maker's head shook side to side from the blow. Vibrations from the hit, traveled up the cane, inflicting a stinging pain in Bert's hands.

"Run! Out the back!" Bert yelled.

The guests took advantage of Bert's sacrifice. Now angered, the Widow Maker's fingers stretched out, wrapping its cold digits around Bert's torso, like rope. Held off the ground by a few feet, the elderly man's legs kicked about. He continued to strike the creature on the arm, with his cane, giving each swing as much strength as he could muster.

Ripping the cane from Bert's hands, the Widow Maker surrounded its fingers around him tighter. Constricting his arms to his lungs, he couldn't move. Breathing was extremely difficult as the Widow Maker's grip pressed against his torso. Bert defiantly spit into the monster's face. However, this didn't faze the horrid creature.

"Slowly beating my song, your body is weak. I will visit again, but the farmer is who I seek."

Al entered the foyer, approaching the Widow Maker, "Let him go."

The Widow Maker released its grasp of Bert. His elderly body painfully ached when he crashed into the hard wood floor. It stared patiently at Al.

"No Al, I'm an old man. You have a son to raise," Bert pleaded.

"His mother will take care of him Bert."

"She's mean to him, Al. Esther will only harm the boy. He needs his father!"

"She's his mother. I do not have a choice. I'm a dead man walking."

"No," Bert whimpered.

The Widow Maker stepped around Bert. Lunging its hands around Al's body, it mocked Bert by singing the chorus to "White Christmas," which continued to blast through the speakers. Blood from Al's body began draining away into a floating mist from his pores. His skin turned milky white. Soon it dried out, withering away, and cracking his skin like the dry riverbed in the desert sand. As Al's dead body was released, the Widow Maker requested his heart. Bert witnessed in horror, as the creature punctured Al's chest open with its claws. Squishing all the way through to the organ, it removed the heart from Al's chest cavity. Untying the chain necklace, it added Al's heart to the collection, by placing it into an empty cage. Blood poured out of the arteries, as the meaty charm, jiggled around its bony neck.

A glowing red portal appeared on the surface of the floor. The Widow Maker jumped inside as it sluggishly closed. Bert crawled over to Al's corpse, weeping silently. Moonlight appeared above Al's body, spotlighting through the foyer's tallest window.

Eerie silence filled the room. The atmosphere became stagnant. Blackened vines creeped down the walls, zigging and zagging until it covered all of the surfaces of the room. Even the furniture, became engulfed in dead vines.

Bert buried his face in the palms of his hands. Depressed, he lost another person important to him. Hannah's voice bounced off the walls of the foyer, removing the silence. Bert quickly scanned his surroundings.

"Mister Bert?" she asked.

"Hannah," he called out, rising slowly to his feet. "Hannah, where are you?"

"I'm here Mister Bert. I've always been around, waiting for my Daddy."

"Let me see you child."

Hannah appeared as a shadow, standing near her father's corpse. "Mister Bones is coming Bert. He's going to take me to my Daddy."

"Hannah, I'm sorry."

"Don't be sorry Mister Bert. It wasn't your fault," she said. Her image became clearer, although only in a poltergeist form. The outline of her body shined like sparkling diamonds. "Mister Bert, you may have to leave. I don't want Mister Bones to take you."

"Who is Mister Bones, honey?

"When the vines show up, so does he."

"Hannah?" the ghostly figure of Al walked towards her.

"Daddy!" she exclaimed, jumping into his arms.

Al's face beamed with joy. "Oh God baby, I didn't think I'd see you again."

"I've always been here Daddy," she cried, holding onto his neck. "Mister Bones is coming Daddy. He'll get us. We have to go."

Just as Hannah predicted, "Mister Bones" arrived. His bony hands was the first aspect Bert noticed, barely visible under his long black sleeves. The cloak revealed a void of nothing under the hood, like a dark cave, without an exit. Mister Bones' height reached the second floor ceiling of the foyer.

"Do not worry Hannah," Al reassured her. "He's here to take us away honey, to a new place. But we're together now. That's all that matters. He'll be back for Junior, then we'll all be together again."

"No!" Bert yelled. "He's not taking Junior!"

A high pitched whispering response, originated from Mister Bones. "You do not have a choice. The Widow Maker will return, to signal my delivery time for Junior."

Slinging his cloak over Al and Hannah, they vanished from Bert's sight. Mister Bones phased out, leaving the room. The vines crept away. The room seemed to be unharmed. Al's body, along with all the destruction, was gone.

# Chapter Three

Crawling to his cane, Bert lifted himself up. He limped to the hallway, passing the study, kitchen, and bathroom, taking a left into a spacious utility room where the back door was located. Pausing, he placed his hand on the electric dryer's surface to steady himself. Quivering, his knees wanted to buckle under. Physically, he was healthy enough to stand, yet his grief wanted to overtake him. Bert commanded himself to file his mourning away. There was nothing he could do to help Al now, but he can check on the others.

Bert exited the door, expecting to be alone, hoping the others escaped. However, to his surprise, he witnessed something completely different. Richey, Olivia, Esther, and a young man, congregated outside on the patio, and yard. Mary wasn't present.

The snow was gone. Freshly cut grass filled Bert's nostrils. Stars filled up the night sky with a full moon perched upon space. The temperature was hot, and muggy. Crickets chirped loudly. Tiki torches, filled with kerosene, lit up brick pathways of the yard.

Esther was seated on a metal patio chair, leaning back from a matching table. A blue and white striped umbrella table, protruded from the middle. Her left hand fingers, were wrapped around a can of diet soda. Streams of smoke waved from her cigarette, resting between the first two digits of her right hand. Esther wore a one piece, yellow bathing suit, with the modest neckline opening above her cleavage. Her hair flowed down her shoulders, in waved ends, parted down the middle of her scalp, teased in volume on both sides. Esther seemed happier than Bert remembered her from before.

Richey was grilling hot dogs, and hamburgers, with ears of buttered corn wrapped in aluminum foil, on a charcoal grill. His hair was thinner on the crown. Large semi-square lenses, filled the frames of his black glasses. Richey wore brown shorts, which reached above his knees, and a plain white undershirt, stained under his armpits.

Richey greeted Bert with a question,"One dog or two Bert?"

"What?" Bert asked perplexed.

"One dog or two? Or do you want a burger and a dog?"

Bert couldn't believe his senses. Just moments before they were all escaping from the Widow Maker, running desperately for their lives. Now, it was as if time had accelerated beyond them.

"I, I don't understand what's going on?"

"Damn Bert," Esther belched. "You losing your mind?"

"Maybe I am," he stated. "Al is dead, Esther. And you're acting like nothing happened."

"That's not fair, Bert. How could you say such an awful thing? Al has been dead for years. We have the right to move on you know. What's wrong with you? You seem confused. Richey and I have been married for five years now."

"Five years? But, Al was just here."

Richey intervened, "Bert, maybe you need to rest. You look like you've been through hell. Rough day or something? Did you take a nasty fall again?"

Ignoring Bert, Esther asked, "Richey, can you hand me another soda from the cooler?"

"You got it hon."

Richey opened up the red cooler near the grill, and delivered the can of soda to Esther. She slapped Richey on the back side.

"I love that ass," she announced.

Bert realized that Richey and Esther were really married. The young man sitting on a bench, next to Olivia in the yard, had to be Junior. Young love permeated their every action. Glances of fiery passion danced in their eyes. Bert recognized that look. It was an expression he had experienced before, young love. Junior placed his hand on her stomach, which was bigger than he remembered. Olivia was pregnant.

Still in disbelief of this state of being, he gazed at the young man. He felt foolish, but he questioned anyhow, "Junior? Is that you?" Yet the young man didn't respond. He and Olivia continued to whisper to each other in a private conversation. Moving his attention to Richey again, he asked, "Where's Mary?"

"Mary? Don't know a Mary."

"But the young woman, Mary, the one whose van had broken down. Is she still here?"

"Sorry Pal, don't know who that is."

"Leave it alone Bert," Esther commanded, with a serious tone.

"No, Esther, I won't leave it alone! What the hell is going on here?"

"You just can't leave shit alone, can you Bert? Always messing things up," Esther stated. The soda in her hand, had disappeared. Instead, a half empty bottle of bourbon whiskey was loosely held.

"Bert, why don't we discuss this like gentlemen?" suggested Richey.

"Gentlemen? I just witnessed a good man get killed by the Widow Maker, and you two are playing house?"

Bert felt a hand squeeze his shoulder from behind. Turning around, Mary was there, looking the same as before. "Bert! We aren't out of the house! It's a trick! It's not real!"

"This could have been a nice peaceful day Bert. Now it's ruined," Esther said. Her voice began to change into a disembodied sound. "Now, the boy must pay! Now the boy, must, die!"

Junior stood up, terrified as his body shrank into a nine year old boy's structure again. Olivia's beaming happiness turned to shambles. Her baby bump deflated. Olivia grabbed Junior's hand. Richey's hair grew thick, his glasses dropped to the floor, and he stumbled ahead, stepping onto his glasses. Richey aged backward to his original form. Each of them, were dressed in the same clothes they arrived in for Christmas dinner.

Stars exploded from the heavens, dropping jagged pieces of glass down upon everyone. Some of the debris sliced through Bert's Santa suit; leaving minor scratches on his face, hands, and arms. The scene around them crumbled, and deteriorated. Pouring down like a bucket of water, the night sky descended quickly.

Walls appeared around them. They were located back inside the den. The room was gloomy. Everyone inside was hunched over, resting on their knees, and covering the back of their heads, to protect themselves from the recently shattered stars of glass. Looking up, Bert witnessed snow falling outside the window. Temperature in the house dropped to frigid. Bert began to shiver.

"Is everyone okay?" Bert asked.

"I'm fine," Richey responded.

"Still here," Mary announced.

"Junior, are you okay?" Richey asked.

Junior's tongue was paralyzed with fear. The young boy felt bewildered, just like everyone else. He remained too petrified to speak.

"He's fine," Olivia said, comforting the boy, by putting her hand on his shoulder. "But, why are we back in the den? The last thing I remember is running toward the back door in the utility room."

"Wait," Bert said, "You don't remember it being hot and muggy outside. Years passing by? All that stuff?"

"I have no clue what you're talking about," Olivia responded. "All I know is, we ran into the utility room, glass began falling from the ceiling, and we appeared here again."

Bert glared at their faces. But someone was missing. "Where's Esther?"

"It's Junior's fault," Esther said with an unearthly tone that echoed loudly off the walls. "The boy must be punished."

Esther was standing in the hallway, just outside the threshold of the den. Still wearing her bathing suit, she removed it. Dropping it to the floor, her nude body was shadowed, with just a hint of moonlight outlining her curves.

"Esther, what are you doing? What's wrong with you?" Richey asked in utter disbelief.

"Like what you see Richey. We could have so much fun together if only that boy wasn't in our lives anymore."

"Esther, you've lost your mind. Leave the boy alone. He's your son for christ sakes. He's not responsible for the death of Hannah, or Al," Bert defended.

Mary grasped onto Bert's bicep. "We have to get out of this house. She's dangerous. Something is not right with her," she stated in a trembling voice.

Richey held onto Junior's hand, pulling him away. "We need to leave, now!"

Richey, Junior, Olivia, and Mary sprinted to the kitchen, heading towards the rear exit. Bert remained behind, too tired, and too bruised, to attempt escape. He stood there, defiantly looking at Esther.

"Al was too good for you Esther. And so is Richey. Leave them be. I'll take care of the boy. Go live your life. Just leave, and never come back."

Stepping towards him, Esther's body began to quiver. Walking into the path of the window, her skin transformed into a hardened insect-like exoskeleton. Red beaming eyes grew larger inside her sockets, creating a circular shape. She dropped to her knees, her hands placed on the hardwood floor. A plated tail pushed out the bottom of her spine, ripping out of her body, swinging, and whipping around. Reaching six feet in length, the end of the tail created the shape of a scorpion stinger. Esther's nose retreated inside her skull, revealing only two nostril holes. Her jaw extended outward nearly twelve inches. When opening her mouth, she let out a painful cough, spewing light chunky vomit onto the floor. Gritting her teeth, they began to fall out, dropping like oval stone pebbles, tapping onto the hardwood floor.

"Help me Bert! Help me!" she screamed, as blood now pooled from her mouth. Heaving like a cat, struggling to cough up a fur ball, a human organ plopped from her mouth, splatting on top of the puke and blood. It was a blackened liver.

Bert took this opportunity for escape, limping as fast as he could through the kitchen, and traveling to the back door. When he arrived, the door was barricaded, boarded, and screwed shut. Circling around through the dining room, he cautiously peeked out into the hallway. Esther wasn't there. So he stumbled, and fumbled his way to the front door. But it too, was blocked with furniture, and boarded down with two by fours.

Olivia whispered near his ear, "Bert!"

Flinching he turned around to face her. "You scared the shit out of me," he mentioned in a hushed tone.

"Up the stairs, come on."

Quietly tiptoeing up the circular staircase, he followed her. They could hear quite a commotion going on in the kitchen as they ascended. Pans clanged against the walls, dishes crashed onto the floor. Something very large thumped against a stationary object.

"Jun-ior!" Esther screamed in anger, trying to locate the boy.

Olivia and Bert reached the second floor, where the others waited in the hallway. Richey was relieved when he saw Bert. "Oh thank God, you found him."

“We have to get out of this house somehow,” Mary said.

“Jun-ior!” Esther’s voice was lurking closer. The group could hear her heavy footsteps nearing the staircase downstairs.

“The attic,” Bert commanded. “Follow me.”

The guests followed Bert into the master bedroom. A stained oak canopy bed, rested in the middle of a honey colored wall. Green silk pillows sat on top of a red, and white sheen comforter. Two night stands matched the bed on each side. The sixty watt bulbs illuminated the lamps, sitting upon the nightstands. Santa and his reindeer, flying above chimneys, were carved into the stone lamps. Green drapes matched the pillows, with a golden sash holding the curtains back. White pristine carpet covered the floor. Two wide windows faced outward into the snowy night sky.

In the corner, another pine Christmas tree stood. The ornaments differed from the one downstairs. Red and green shiny bows were peppered all around. A blinking gold star remained on top of the tree. Poinsettia garland wrapped around the tree. Four presents wrapped in brown paper, and twine bows tied all four sides of each gift.

The attic door, matched the colors of the wall, with a faded brass handle, and antique key hole below. Bert shuffled over to his large oak dresser, and opened a top drawer. He pulled out a skeleton key.

“The attic locks from the inside and outside. We can hide in the attic until morning. Maybe it will be gone by then.”

"What happened to my Mom?" Junior asked, breaking his silence.

Mary answered, "She's sick. I'm sure she'll feel better soon. She wanted us to take care of you, for now."

"I don't like attics. They're creepy and full of ghosts."

"Don't worry," Richey reassured, "We'll be with you. You won't be alone. Maybe we'll play some games? Wouldn't that be fun Junior?"

"Yes," he answered hesitantly.

Bert unlocked the attic door, "I have chests up there with sheets and blankets. It'll be like a slumber party, Junior."

"Okay," the boy spoke softly.

Bert opened the door for everyone to enter up the tightly spaced steps. One by one they filed in. Each roughly texture step creaked as their weight shifted upon them. Bert closed the door behind him, and locked it. His knees created a cracking noise with each step he ascended, almost as loudly, as the old stairs themselves.

# Chapter Four

The attic was slightly colder than the rest of the house. Gusts of wind pounded against the roof. A small dirty window was located towards the gabled end of the attic. Rafters angled upwards, allowing sufficient headroom in the middle in the area. Pink insulation was pressed and stapled, covered over by a layer of clear plastic, between the spacing. Cobwebs sprawled around the peaks of the ceiling. Rough sheathing, covered the floors, with layers of dust, revealing the recent footprints of the guests.

Four cardboard boxes, sealed with packing tape, were stacked against the perimeter of the room. Three antique round topped chests, were placed on the opposite sides of the window. However, only the outlines of these objects could be viewed from the glass, dusting the room with just enough light to see basic shapes.

Too frightened to speak, the remainder of the guests, and Bert, tiptoed softly, gingerly sitting on the dusty floor. Esther, or what was perceived to be a monstrous version of her, made her footsteps known on the floor beneath them. Picture frames could be heard falling off the walls below. With the collaboration of the powerful wind outside, and the scorpion-like creature violently wrecking the rooms inside, the house shook with angry vibrations.

But soon the quivering structure ceased movement. Esther could be heard stomping down the steps. The last sound was possibly the front door being bashed out. It was hoped, that the creature left the premises.

"I think it's gone. Maybe we can leave now," Olivia suggested.

"No, whatever that thing is, it could be waiting for us to go outside. I say we stay here until morning light," Bert suggested.

"What makes you think it will be safer by morning?" asked Richey.

"I don't know honestly. It's just a feeling. At least we'll be able to see things clearer. I'm just hoping it'll be gone by then."

"It will be gone? That's my mom,"Junior defended her.

"That's not your mother. I don't know where she is, but that monster is just disguised as her. I'm sure your mother is somewhere else, Junior. We'll find her after it is safe."

Junior nodded, sitting on the floor, pulling his knees up to his chest. He wrapped his arms around his shins. Resting his head on top of his knees, the boy was sadly quiet.

"It's awfully cold up here," Mary pointed out.

"Right you are, let me find some light first." Bert walked delicately over toward the window sill. Near the corner of that same wall, a red oil lamp rested on top of a stool. "Anyone have a lighter?"

"I do," Mary replied pulling a pink lighter from her front pant pocket.

"Me too," Richey confirmed with a silver flip top lighter in his hands.

Bert received the lighter from Mary, and removed the clear glass, lamp chimney. Rotating the knob, the wick pushed upward. He lit it, and returned the chimney to surround the flame. "Good thing it's full of kerosene. Mary, would you be a dear and find something to cover the window? We don't want that thing seeing the light." Mary found an antique oil painting of a fox hunt, and leaned it against the wall, covering the window. "Everyone, please sift through those chests for sheets and blankets. We need to keep warm."

Two of the chests were stacked full of bed coverings. They smelled musty, but at least it would keep them warmer. As the remaining guests began to wrap themselves up, Mary searched though the third chest. The lid creaked when opening. Her eyes lit up with curiosity. Old photo albums were stacked inside.

"Bert, do you mind if I look at your photos? I like old photos."

"Go ahead, there should be another oil lamp near, where I got the last one. Why don't you go ahead and light it?"

"Can I look at them Mister Bert?" Junior asked.

"By all means, help yourself Junior."

After Mary lit the lamp, she leaned her back against the heavy chest, stretching out her legs on the floor. Junior seated himself next to her. Richey, Olivia, and Bert found some scattered, wooden kitchen chairs, and placed them next to the fox hunt painting.

Richey suggested, "We need a plan Bert. Just in case that thing gets up here."

"I'm working on it. Nothing comes to mind right now. I just need a little more time."

Olivia stared down to the floor, distracted. Her mind wasn't in the here and now. All hope fluttered from her expression. While Bert and Richey attempted to discuss options, she pulled her sleeve up and focused on the purple bruises around her wrists.

"What the hell is that?" Richey asked, referencing her bruises. "Who did that to you?"

"It's nothing."

"The hell it is, " Richey followed up.

"I fell down the steps."

"Don't lie to us, Olivia, those are pressured finger marks," Bert stated.

"It's my fault. I didn't listen. I'm not a good person."

"Olivia, yes you are," Bert consoled. "Who did this to you?"

"My father."

"Why would your father do this to you? You don't even live with him."

"It's a long story," her bottom lip began to shake. "I don't want to talk about it right now."

Bert stood up, and walked over to her, putting his hand on her shoulder, he said, "Okay, we don't have to talk about this now. We've got enough to worry about at the moment. But we're here for you if you need us. And after this night, we'll need to address this. We'll keep you safe."

"Thanks," she smiled, but it seemed like a forced gesture of disbelief.

Changing the subject, Bert mentioned, "I think I got some bourbon up here."

"That's more like it," Richey agreed. "Where is it Bert? I'll get it."

"It's in a wooden crate on the opposite end. Here," Bert said handing him the oil lamp, "You'll need this to see it in the dark."

Richey found an unopened bottle of Kentucky Bourbon, and a few dirty plastic cups. Returning to them, he wiped out the inside of the cups with his shirt. "Sorry, it's a little dusty. But at least the alcohol will kill the germs," he giggled. Pouring the dark golden liquid into the cups, he handed them to Bert and Olivia.

Bert raised his cup, Olivia and Richey did the same. "To Al, the best man I've ever known. I will miss you," he said with a fading voice, and glassy eyes.

"To Al," Richey replied.

"To Al," Olivia joined.

Bert glanced over to Junior. The boy leaned his head on Mary's shoulder, as they sifted through the pictures. He wondered how the kid was coping so well with such a devastating turn of events.

Tapping their cups together, they doused the bourbon back to their throats, gulping the shot down. "Another one?" Bert asked feeling like his chest was burning from the inside.

Richey replied with an enthusiastic, but whispered, "Damn right."

***

Slight inebriation affected Bert, Olivia, and Richey's senses. From their stressful night, the alcohol calmed their nerves enough to slow down the sense of panic. A glimmering idea finally arrived in Bert's thoughts.

"I got it," Bert announced in low volume.

"Got what?" asked Richey.

"I know what we should do. If we hear that thing crashing around inside the second floor of the house again, we can start climbing out, and down the attic window."

"That is an extremely long way down," Olivia mentioned. "And in no offense to you, you're not exactly a young man."

"Yes, I realize that, but what is our other options. We have a plethora of extra sheets, and blankets. We can tie them together to make a temporary rope, and lower ourselves down. We can strap it to one of vertical studs in the unfinished attic walls."

"I like it better than sitting here, hoping that thing won't show up," Richey agreed.

Richey and Bert began constructing a rope made from cotton sheets, tying each segment together. Using tightly tripled knots, the rope was nearly finished. But Mary noticed something peculiar in the photo album she was perusing.

"Bert, I think you need to see this," she interrupted, with a look of uneasiness.

"In a minute Mary, we're working on our escape."

"I don't know how to explain this. Please, just for a second. it's important."

Bert was annoyed by her insistence, but gave in to it. "Okay, let me see what's so pressing."

Mary handed Bert a folded newspaper clipping. He unfolded it, and proceeded to inspect it. Inside was an obituary from a local paper which read:

*Esther Joanna Washington*

*Esther expired from cirrhosis of the liver on December 24th, 1968 at 2:35 AM. She was found deceased, by her husband, Richard S. Washington, outside their home on Mulberry Lane. Her ashes will be put to rest in the Claymore Cemetery, on December 28th, 1968 at 11:00 AM. Only gravesite funeral services can be attended. The family requests that in lieu of flowers, those paying their respects should provide monetary donations to the Homeless Housing Fund of the Claymore Baptist Church on 30th Street.*

"Mulberry Lane? Richey?" Bert questioned, with a puzzled expression.

"What?" Richey inquired.

"You better look at this."

Richey read the obituary, with his mouth drooped open in astonishment. "It, it says Esther was my wife? She died here, on Mulberry Lane? This house? Alright, now I'm officially freaked out."

"You mean, the fact that we have demons running amok in the house, didn't freak you out?" Olivia asked.

"Of course it does, but why does it say this?"

"And why does it say it happened decades ago," Mary concluded.

Richey replied, "Decades ago? What do you mean, it's not…"

"Mama's dead?" Junior asked, interrupting, on the precipice of weeping aloud.

Bert attempted to defuse the situation, and keep Junior's voice down. "No Junior, it's just a fake, joke paper. I know Esther is fine."

The floor shook beneath their feet like small earthquake tremors. The sound of something large hitting the walls beneath them echoed, up to the attic.

"It's coming back. Quick, we need to get down the window now. Mary, you go first. Then we'll send Junior down the rope, just in case you need to catch him, should he fall," Bert commanded.

Bert tied the end of the sheet rope around a vertical web stud, and Richey held the sheet rope, stabilizing Mary's decent out the window. It stopped short just five feet from the ground. She called up to the window, "Send him down!"

Closer and closer the sound of thumping footsteps grew louder. Bert helped Junior through the window, while Richey steadied the rope.

"I'm too scared," Junior admitted.

"Don't worry, Mary will be there to catch you if you fall. But you're a strong boy, you can climb down. Just like climbing down a tree, but much easier."

"Okay," he confirmed. "I can do this, I've climbed trees before."

Richey walked closer towards the window while gripping the rope, so he could lower the boy down at a safe pace. Junior jumped the remainder of the way down, landing safely on his feet, dropping to the snowy ground.

The attic entrance door bursted outward, exploding up the steps of the room. Puke, with chunks of food, and blood, splattered against the floor, protruding from segments between hardened insect creature's body. The neck of the monster, snaked up the steps, connected to Esther's deformed, and grotesque head. The head extended further into the room. Red eyes scanned the attic, locating Bert, Richey, and Olivia. They stood still, knowing the time for fleeing had passed.

"Jun-iorrrrr, where is, Jun-iorrrrrrr?" Esther asked.

"Far away from you!" Bert screamed.

"Outsssssssiiiiiidddddde," Esther croaked. Her head, and neck, whipped away from them, and pulled back to the scorpion-like body, inside Bert's bedroom, down the short attic steps.Vibrating walls shook and banged, as it moved through the second floor, and journeyed downstairs.

"We have to protect the boy!" Richey exclaimed. He grabbed the half empty bottle of Kentucky bourbon, and sprinted down, out where the door used to be located.

Bert and Olivia jogged behind him. His arthritic bones did their best to stabilize themselves. His cane stomped loudly with every step. Descending the second floor, and outside to the porch, where the front doors used to be; Richey was far away from Bert's sight. Following the footprints, and insect-like stab patterns in the snow, he trekked to the side of the large house.

The creature chased after Mary and Junior. Richey followed behind, along with Olivia, and then came to a halt. Bert could see Richey, pulling out a handkerchief from his coat pocket. Pushing the cloth down into the opening of the bourbon, he kept a portion of it sticking out the spout of the glass bottle.

Mary tripped, and stumbled onto the ground, accidentally pulling Junior along with the drop. Richey lit the handkerchief, with his silver lighter, creating a molotov cocktail.

"Esther!" he screamed out. The creature turned around, distracted by Richey's exclaim. "Have another drink you bitch!"

Heaving the bottle with all his might, the explosive bomb landed on the creature's back. Igniting into flames, Esther screeched. Fire engulfed her. The scorpion tale reached out, whipping uncontrollably, penetrating Junior's chest with the stinger. The boy cried out from the extreme pain of his wound. Esther backed off, and rolled around in the snow, but the fire couldn't be extinguished. Like a bonfire, smoke filled the sky. The stench of burning flesh and sewage almost made Bert vomit. Esther's bug-like corpse roasted, melting the snow around her. The body ceased motion, lying still as the flames continued to blaze.

Richey, Bert, and Olivia finally reached Mary and Junior's location. The boy was bleeding through his clothes. He was stricken unconscious. Mary held pressure on the wound.

"We gotta get the boy to the hospital," Richey confirmed, picking up the boy. "Let's go!" Trotting through the ankle deep snow, they reached the driveway. Approaching a creme and wood grained exterior, of a Ford Fairmont Squire, Richey commanded, "Mary, get in the back seat and hold onto Junior."

"Wait, whose car is this?" Bert asked.

Richey ignored Bert's question, and they began entering the vehicle. Richey inserted the key and fired up the engine, while Bert climbed into the front passenger seat. Olivia entered the passenger side, rear door. Olivia rested Junior's head on her lap, while his feet stretched across Mary.

It wasn't pressing concern as of now, but Bert couldn't understand why Richey had keys to this car. He was sure that Richey was driving a different car, earlier that night. Where did this car come from?

Richey was switching gears, pushing the gas pedal as far to the floor as possible. Silent Night blasted aloud through the car radio speakers. Richey turned down the music volume knob. Yet, the level of volume didn't change. Speeding as fast as he could on the icy roads, in the darkness, Bert began to worry.

"Richey, slow down! You're gonna get us in an accident before we get to the hospital," Bert warned.

"Shut up Bert! I know what I'm doing. The boy isn't going to make it unless…"

"Deer!" Olivia exclaimed while pointing.

Time seemed to slow down in Bert's mind. The buck stood helpless in front of them, too frightened to escape the trajectory. Richey's vehicle struck the animal. The impact caused the sound of a booming thump, as the deer's carcass flew over the hood, and crashed into the windshield. The tires swerved out of control, skidding along the path of the icy road. When the deer fell off the hood, the busted windshield revealed a tall oak tree, speeding towards them. Bert's vision beheld a transformation to darkness. Crushing metal, and shattering glass, filled his eardrums. And then, he was surprised by a jolt to his body, as it whipped forward, and snapped back from the safety belt.

# Chapter Five

"Bert!" Mary exclaimed, shaking the old man, persistent in waking him.

"I think he's coming to," Olivia commented. "Oh God! Oh God! No!"

Bert could hear their voices trembling. Opening his eyelids, his vision blurred, and his brain pounded with a hammering headache. It was hard to breathe, like the being punched in the stomach. Bert took short quick breaths, but tried to remain calm.

Olivia and Mary began to wail. He turned his head towards their direction, they were standing outside the car. They were too frightened to approach any closer. Bert reached over to Richey's shoulder, closing his eyes to gain some sort of relief from his headache.

"Richey, are you okay?" Bert asked. Opening his eyelids again, his vision cleared. "Oh God, Richey?"

Richey's body slumped over the steering wheel. His skull was smashed into it. The wheel penetrated into his forehead, with a crevice revealing his exposed brain matter. Blood covered his face, oozing down the steering wheel, and puddling onto the floor mats.

"Is he? Is he?" Mary stammered.

Bert's lip quivered uncontrollably. Holding back tears, replying as his voice cracked, "Yes." Bert was sad, but mainly angry. After surviving an otherworldly encounter, a 'goddamn deer killed my friend,' he thought. "Help me out," Bert asked the two women while unbuckling his safety belt. Each grabbed him gently by the hands, and elbows, assisting him as he twisted to get to his feet. Reaching down to pick up his cane, Bert wanted to scream from the immense agony he felt in his back, and hips. But held back from outburst, like a young man full of strength could. Bert asked, "Where is Junior?"

"I…I don't know," Mary responded. "When we woke, he was gone."

Bert removed his cell phone from his pocket; still no signal. "Let's follow his tracks." In the snow, the boy's footprints dragged through, leaving two lines heading into the woods. They followed along. "I don't see any blood in the snow. He's probably okay."

Mary was sniffling, holding back her sadness for a stranger she just met. Olivia trailed behind. Just a few moments earlier, she was emotional about Richey's death. But now, her expression lacked any feeling at all. Her eyes simply gazed down at her feet, but she continued to follow along.

Further behind she slowed. Bert and Mary stopped, for Olivia to catch up. "Olivia, we got to find Junior. Time is of the essence, it is cold. The boy must be found," Bert commanded.

Looking up, she gave him a blank stare. "Why Bert?"

"What do you mean, 'why?'"

"We're all going to die anyway Bert. Even the boy won't make it. There's no use in fighting anymore."

"What do you suggest we do Olivia? Sit here in the snow, freeze to death?"

"Yes," she replied, dropping to her knees in the snow, then curling down, resting her back against a maple tree.

Bert moved over to Olivia, consoling her by putting his right hand on her left shoulder, "My dear, there is so much more life to live. Please, we need your help. If not for yourself, do it for us, do it for Junior. The boy is lost, cold, and probably frightened out of his mind. His father is dead, his mother is dead, and his sister is dead; we are all that boy has left. If we don't make it past tonight, at least we gave it our best effort, and that has got to be worth something."

Olivia looked up into Bert's tired eyes and conceded, "Okay Bert, we'll find the boy."

Mary marched over, and held out her hand to Olivia. She grasped onto Mary's grip, and heaved herself up. The air felt colder by the minute.

Reaching deeper into the woods, after ten minutes of following the footsteps, they halted. The tracks stopped in a small clearing. But Junior wasn't there.

"Where could he be?" Mary asked.

"Quiet, hold your breath for a moment, please." They complied. Bert heard heavy breathing, as if someone was sleeping. Nearly twenty feet from them, Junior laid still in the snow. "Over there!" Bert, Olivia, and Mary jogged over to the boy. He knelt down over Junior to feel the pulse on his neck. "His heart's still beating. Let's get him back to the road. Hopefully, we'll be able to flag down a car."

"Why is it, that he didn't have any tracks near him?" Olivia asked.

"Good question, the only thing I can figure, is that he was thrown."

"Twenty feet? Who could have thrown him that far?"

"Listen I can't explain it, and nor do I care right now. We need to head back to the road."

"What was that?!" Mary exclaimed in a fright.

Bert scanned the landscape around them. "What was what? I didn't see anything. Wait! I just saw something too."

Out of the corner of Bert's eye, a dark shadow passed from tree to tree. Shifting his attention to the direction of movement, two more shadows appeared. Three, four, five, six, forms multiplied from the original shadow's form. Shapes of humans with inconsistent body outlines surrounded them. None of their forms reached the ground, only black masses of smoke, encircled them in the moonlight. Bert's heart began to pump faster. Fifteen to twenty spirits blocked every path of escape.

"We'll take the boy," they all whispered in unison. "He belongs to us."

"No! You will not!" Bert screamed back at them.

But none of them could stop the ghostly figures. Instantly, they all formed into one. With lightning speed, the shadow scooped up Junior. At a sprinting pace, the smoky spirit carried the boy's body, nearly fifty feet away from them. Junior's arms flopped around like dangling ropes in a sea storm.

Bert, Olivia, and Mary took off in brave pursuit. Eventually, the shadowed ghost speeded too far off in the distance. Mary and Olivia were nearly one hundred and fifty yards ahead of Bert. His aging body tried desperately to keep up. Soon they were lost from his sight. The snowflakes sped up their rate of descent, helping to mask their location in the thickening woods.

He was alone in the tall grass, almost at the position of another tree line. His hands cramped up from the bitter freeze. Bert's fingers clawed upward. He could barely move his digits.

High pitched whispers carried voices, with every gust of wind. "Berrrrrttttt, don'ttttt you reeememberrrrr usssssss?"

"What do you want from me?!" Bert asked, raising his tone.

"Bert!" a quick one syllable blurt penetrated his right ear. He ducked down, out of instinct, like the reaction from gunfire. Yet, no one could be viewed near him. Cackling laughter, swirled around his head. The mocking giggles of male spirits filled the night sky.

***

"Move your ass Private!" a soldier dressed in army green roared. He was a young man, aged in his early twenties. Covered in mud, an outer netting surrounded his helmet, stuffed full of twigs. The soldier's left arm was missing. Human flesh swayed, dripping just below his shoulder. "I said move it!"

"Sarge, your arm!" Bert exclaimed over the tick and tock gunfire around him. He was surrounded by an agricultural field of rice patties. The humidity felt like a sauna.

"Forget my arm! Move it!"

Bert began rushing away, obeying the injured soldier's command. An M-60 appeared into existence, in Bert's young, unwrinkled hands. His right finger rested beside the trigger. Bert felt the heavy load of a backpack, strapped to his torso. Rain began flooding down like buckets of water. Other soldiers in his platoon, were far ahead of him. He began to forget the present time period, and relived a pivotal moment of his tour, in Vietnam.

Bert chugged straight ahead, but peered back, just once, to see his Sergeant get blown up by mortar rounds, exploding like fireworks of death. Men around him began to drop. Bloody mists sprayed from bullet holes entering them. He felt a scolding sensation enter, his left calf. An enemy bullet had entered his body. Bert yelped out, dropping down in the muddy waters, of rice patties, fertilized with a mix of human, and cow feces. The stench made Bert dry heave.

Bert was close to a foxhole, that he and another soldier dug up, earlier in the day. The small trench was located past the last rice patty, on an incline to drier land, behind the jungle line of trees, and brush. Crawling through the muck, using his arms, and right leg, he dropped down inside. He fell upon two corpses of men from his platoon. On one of the bodies, he removed the belt from his waist. Wrapping the belt above his wound, he pulled it tight. Bert's hands glistened with the shine of fresh blood, pouring from his leg.

The battle continued on, as United States soldiers in other foxholes, continued to burst out rounds, towards the lights of enemy gun fire, hidden in the trees past the clearing. Night was inching closer. The stars spread across the infinite expanse.

Bert knew time was against him, before he bled out. Reaching into his front pocket, behind his cigarettes, was a silver lighter. Flipping the top open, he ignited the flame. Placing one end of the belt between his teeth, he kept the other end wrapped around his wound. Taking a deep breath, his teeth clinched down onto the belt, grunting loudly as he seared his gunshot. Bert had to hold the flame stationary, until he smelled the slight burn of flesh. Bert's eyes rolled backward, he passed out from agony.

***

Bert woke to the absence of sound. The battle was over, which left uncertainty as to who he was surrounded by, friend or foe? It was eerily quiet. Poking his head out of the trench, he could see the patties ahead, filled with dead soldiers from both nations. A few yards away, a man in his platoon, was lying on his back, still breathing, resting near a tree line. Climbing out of the hole, Bert crawled slowly over to him, on his stomach.

"Miller?"

Miller Jones was covered with a mix of fresh, and coagulated blood. His face was pale, from the drainage of precious life fluid. He compressed his hand to the wound his right side, below his ribs. "B…Bert, help me."

"Help is on the way buddy."

"N..No Bert," Miller said. "Charlie is…coming closer."

Bert listened. He could hear the faintest of voices on the other side of the field of rice. They were speaking Vietnamese. "Shit, we gotta hide. You're coming with me."

Miller was thin in body frame, and short in height, which was a positive advantage for transporting him away. Bert gripped Miller by the back collar, dragging him along, and crawling on his hands and knees. Reaching the foxhole,

Bert assisted Miller to rest upright, to prevent any choking of blood.

"You're wasting… your time… Bert… I'm… a… dead… man," he said, pausing between breaths. His lungs created a wheezing, low leveled squeak.

"No, you and I are getting out of here. There's supposed to be another platoon sent to our location. We just didn't expect Charlie to be here earlier than expected. But our boys will be here, just hold tight."

Miller reached into his breast pocket, pulling out a folded letter. "I wrote this… yesterday… I want… you to… give it to… my family… when you… get home."

"You can tell them in person."

"No Bert… I'm a dead man… I'm losing blood… by the… second."

Bert could see that Miller was serious. His face reflected a pale violet hue. Miller Jone's appearance, resembled a talking cadaver. "Alright, I promise. I'll take it to them," he conceded.

"The… address… is… on… the back. Th… Thank… you," Miller smiled, his mouth filling up with darkened red liquid, pouring down his chin, and staining his teeth pink.

"Stay with me Miller. Miller?"

Bert felt under his jaw to feel for a pulse. Faintly throbbing, Miller's body was holding on longer than his will to live. Bert reached back, and slapped him across the cheek.

"Goddammit Bert! I…I'm… tryin'… to die… here. Give me… peace."

"Hell no."

The Viet Cong were fast approaching to their position, just several yards away. Miller suggested to Bert in a whisper, "The bodies… hide… under… the bodies."

Bert quickly pulled one of the fallen soldiers on top of Miller, then grabbed another, positioning himself underneath his fallen brother in arms. Soon, the enemies were looking down into their foxhole. Bert couldn't understand what they were saying, due to their difference in language.

But soon, the Viet Cong soldier motioned his bayonet over the corpse atop of him. Bert remained silent, holding his breath, praying the enemy wouldn't pierce him. Reaching back ever so slightly, the enemy soldier was about to stab the dead soldier on top. Pop! Pap! Pop! The enemy soldier's head exploded, splattering brains, and bone fragments onto Bert. His carcass dropped on top of Bert. Crimson colored blood poured onto Bert's face, and mouth.

"Fuck you!" Miller screamed, holding an abandoned M-60. With a last surge of adrenaline, Miller stood. He began firing at the enemies rushing to the sound of gunfire. Miller was gunned down in a hail of bullets. Stumbling back, he dropped on top of the man he just killed. Now, Bert had three bodies resting, on top of him.

Breathing was hindered from the weight pressing against him. Yet, he inhaled short breaths of air. More gunfire ensued, as reinforcements of U.S. soldiers finally arrived to engage the enemy. Bert knew he was saved. He was the only man left alive in his platoon.

***

Bert looked up to a neglected farmhouse, out of place for a jungle setting. In fact, the jungle wasn't there altogether. He was on the edge of a forest full of pine, oak, and maple, growing around the property. Bert stared at his hands, full of darkened age spots, and wrinkly skin. His body was aged again. The cane rested beside him. Standing his cane upright, he pulled himself up, with both hands gripping the handle. Olivia and Mary caught up to him.

"Bert, how did you run so fast? You sprinted past us." Mary panted.

"Adrenaline, I guess?" he responded, temporarily dumbfounded by the events he relived. "I think Junior is in this farmhouse."

Mary stared at the dilapidated ruins of a home and asked, "Are you sure?"

"Yes," Bert confirmed with confidence.

The house stood two stories high, with a barn style roof. Rotten wood shingles, drooped inside the partially collapsed center section of the roof. Faded and cracked, white paint covered the exterior. Most of the windows were broken, with vines growing in, and out of them, reaching the second floor. Nature had reclaimed the home.

Bert's legs wobbled from exhaustion. Mary strolled closely, alongside him, to ensure he wouldn't fall. "You're a good kid Mary," he complimented her. "Thank you for looking out for me tonight."

"Don't mention it."

Olivia dragged her feet slowly behind them. She couldn't escape her melancholy expressions and thoughts. When they reached the porch, suffering from a state of extreme deterioration, a gum tree sprouted between the cracked concrete steps. The front door was partially ajar, but vines held it stationary. Mary pushed with all her might. Bert assisted her, as the hinge screws pulled out of the softened wood. The door crashed to the floor, almost causing them to stumble with it.

"This place, seems familiar," Bert emphasized. "This was Al's home."

"That's impossible, how could they live in a place like this? We just saw Al and Esther tonight," Mary voiced.

"I don't know, but I am not mistaken. I know this house. It used to be beautiful."

"Well, we can figure that out later. Right now, I can't see anything," Mary stated.

"I know where the candles are, wait here." Bert knew the layout of the house very well. Atop the fireplace mantle, was a series of wax candles. He returned to Mary, and Olivia, with three red candles. He asked Mary, "Do you still have that lighter?" Mary pulled out the same plastic, pink lighter from earlier. Bert lit the candles, and handed one to each person. The two remaining guests nodded in thanks. "The wax will get hot, but it won't burn you. Wrap your sleeve around your hands, and hold onto the candle, if the wax drip is too uncomfortable for you.

"Now what," asked Mary, shivering from the lack of a coat.

"Here, take this," he said, stripping off his Santa coat and handing it over to Mary. The old man had a black sweater underneath.

"But, you'll be too cold."

"I'll be fine. I had three layers of tops on anyhow. Besides, I like the cold weather. I feel regret that I didn't offer it to you earlier. I wasn't thinking correctly."

"Thank you Bert."

"Don't mention it. Now, both of you stay behind me while we check the house."

Bert stretched out the candle ahead of him. Entering the kitchen, the boards creaked. Moss hung from the ceiling. Snow had drifted onto the wooden counter tops, filling up the antique sink with ice. Roots from the trees, grew into the bottoms of the walls, covering the corners, and penetrating the cabinets.

"Bert, this place has to have been empty for many decades. I still don't understand. How could Al and Esther live here?" Mary asked.

"This whole night doesn't make any sense, Mary. Everything is topsy turvy. This all feels familiar, yet foreign at the same instance. All I know is, I have to save Junior."

The group searched every room on the bottom floor. They checked the bathroom, the closets, and the living room again. Bert noticed a barren Christmas tree, with three crushed gifts beneath. He didn't recall the tree being there when they first entered. Junior wasn't located on the first floor, so Bert led them to the staircase. Cracked and rotting steps, bent as they put their weight on it. Ascending three steps, then turning right, up ten more, they reached the second floor.

Peeling flower wallpaper, rolled down major sections of the hallway. It was too narrow of space for all three to walk beside each other. In a single file, they entered the first bedroom to the left. It was Hannah's former room. A small metal bed rested in the corner. Rats and other vermin, had ripped apart the mattress over the years. The stuffing of the bed piled on the surface, and pieces were scattered around the floor beside it. A wooden dresser, painted yellow, was situated on the opposite side of the room. Bert walked over to it, and picked up an ivory brush, with horse hair bristles, next to the mirror caked with dust. Strands of ginger curls, could still be viewed between the bristles.

"Hannah's brush," he confirmed, placing it back down. "Let's go to Junior's room."

Stepping back to the hallway, they entered the second bedroom, to the left. It too was abandoned. Junior's bed was near a closed window, with dirty blue curtains. The mattress was missing. Another yellow dresser, matched Hannah's, with the exception of a mirror missing from the surface.

"Well, he's not here, " Olivia pointed out.

"Yes, yes, I know." Bert strolled over to the dresser, and opened up the top drawer of three. He reached inside, and pulled out a catcher's mitt, and a baseball. "This looks so familiar. I've seen this before."

"Bert," Mary intervened. "We're here for Junior, not a trip down memory lane."

Bert agreed, replying, "Of course, my dear. You're right. Let's check Al and Esther's room." However, Bert didn't return the baseball, he stuck it in his loose, right pant leg pocket, of his red Santa pants.

Crossing the hallway, they entered the master bedroom. Walking through abandoned cobwebs, they tracked fresh footprints, onto the layers of dust on the surface floor. This full bed frame, made from dark stained wood, was missing a mattress also. Years of deterioration, and neglect, caused the frame to collapse.

However, an anomaly caught Olivia's attention."Bert, over here, " she called out, waving her hand towards him. "Look at this nightstand."

The nightstand was freshly dusted. Lemon scents wafted from fresh dusting wax. Three pictures in silver frames were buffed and shined. Bert used his candle, to peer closely at the colorless photographs. One of them was the image of Al, and Esther, standing in front of a church, on their wedding day. Beaming smiles stretched across their expressions, while staring into the camera lens. Their happiness seemed genuine.

A grouped family photo, rested behind the glass on the second frame. Hannah sat atop Al's shoulders, both giggling. Junior hugged his mother around her waist. Al's rickety old truck could be seen in the background, behind the farmhouse they were currently inside.

Olivia's eyes grew wider once they all studied the third frame. In the picture, Simmons wore his army service uniform. His right arm was wrapped around a beautiful woman, in a large printed flower dress. Olivia, was the woman in the picture.

"What the hell is going on? Olivia, why are you in this picture?" Bert asked, turning around to her.

With a stone cold, and empty expression, she ignored Bert, but spoke to Mary. "Don't you know me Mary? Don't you know who I am? Don't you recognize me?"

"I…I can't remember."

"She's not worth remembering Mary," Simmons interrupted, entering the room from a second door. "Olivia only cares about one person, herself."

"Simmons? Where have you been? I was worried about you."

"Bert, I've always been here. I've been with you all night."

"What are you talking about?"

Simmons chose to disregard Bert's question, directing his attention to Olivia instead. "Just die Olivia! Isn't that what you want to do anyway? Isn't it the truth, Olivia? You judge all men like him. No matter how many times your father beat you, you always loved him more didn't you? I couldn't even touch you, without you thinking of him! This whole situation is screwed up! I tried so hard to rescue you. I used to see the marks he left behind. Yet, you chose to still love a man that raped you repeatedly! You gave him the power to run your life. It's almost as if you enjoyed him, more than you did us? You're nothing, but a selfish bitch! Just like my mother!"

"You are your mother. Just another damned drunk!" Olivia screamed at the top of her lungs.

"You made me drink. Living with you was hell." Simmons' jaw dropped open. The skin on his face was blanched, just like Bert remembered earlier that night. Veins pulsed again, in his neck, and face. Blood ran down his mouth as the long whipping tongue revealed itself. His eyes became a void, dark as coal.

Bert pulled the baseball from his pocket, and hurled it towards Simmons' head. Distracting Simmons' attention from Olivia, Bert yelled, "Run Olivia! Run!"

But Olivia just stood there, motionless, with the look of apathy. Simmons' right arm stretched out, revealing blackened leathery skin, wrapping around Bert, and Mary, like a tight rubber band. They were unable to break free.

"Nothing hurts like a sharp tongue," Simmons spoke in a low pitch, but just enough for everyone to hear. "Merry Christmas to me I guess. You ruined us both. What waste you turned out to be."

Olivia pulled up her sleeves, exposing the bruises on her arms. Simmons' tongue whipped up her left forearm, slicing a vertical wound. Then the razored tongue snapped down her right forearm. Blood poured out of her arms like water in a spigot, puddling on the dusty floor. The blood mixed with the dirt, as it floated on top. Olivia collapsed. Her flesh deteriorated quickly, until nothing was left, except her bone foundation.

Mary and Bert were too shocked to cry out. Simmons released his grip from them. His body began to shrink. Smaller and smaller, he transformed into a child. Simmons was actually Junior.

"I'm sorry. I didn't mean to hurt her. I didn't mean it," Junior cried. Sprinting away, Junior escaped the room, but on his way out, he kicked over Olivia's candle that she dropped. The flame remained, and landed onto the dry curtains. It immediately ignited into an inferno, spreading quicker than a natural fire, engulfing the wall.

"We have to leave!" Bert called out in a panic.

Bert and Mary hustled down the stairs, and out the front door. Now, nearly forty feet away, they stopped for breath. Gazing at the abandoned farmhouse, as flames accelerated faster, covering the entire house. An explosion from an exposed gas line shook the area. Wood and glass splintered towards them. Bert tackled Mary to the icy ground. He shielded Mary, as best he could.

# Chapter Six

Mary didn't wake. Bert tried to shake her. He placed his two forefingers, under her jaw line against the neck, to check for a pulse. She was still alive. The moonlight revealed a tiny bit of blood, on the back of her head. Penetrated in her skull, was a fragment of wood, no bigger than three quarters of an inch. Bert chose not to remove the shrapnel, for if he did, she may bleed out from the wound.

The fire from the farmhouse illuminated her skin in an orange tone. Although the initial blast was very hot, the inferno was too far away to feel the warmth now. If they were to survive the night, Bert knew they couldn't let their body temperatures drop too low.

Every motion he tried to attempt, felt like a pins and needles, stabbing all over his body. Slowly rising to his feet, he knelt over to grab her by the wrists. Bert's body felt heavier, and keeping his balance proved to be a complicated task. Pulling her nearly fifteen feet closer to the fiery home, he soon felt the heat warming his clothes. Involuntarily falling down, he landed beside Mary. Curling his knees to his chest, he yelped. Agonizing shocks traveled from his neck, and shot down to his feet.

He lost so many people that night. Friends that he loved. Even Esther, had her good points, until she lost her mind after the death of her daughter, Hannah.

Bert could hear Hannah's laughter with the frigid breeze. Tiny running thumps on the ground seemed to travel behind him. Every time he tried to catch a glimpse of the small footsteps, he was disappointed. Juvenile giggles of children playing "hide and go seek" faded away slowly. Soon, the only noise, was the wail of wind.

None of this made sense to him. Either he was losing his mind, or this strange night of horror, was true. 'It feels real. This wet snow is real. That fire, is real. Mary is real. Isn't she? This physical agony, is definitely not a hoax!' He convinced himself.

Reaching into his left pocket, he pulled out his cell phone. It was damp, from the cold night, and melting snow against his apparel. Bert gazed at the fogged screen, while remaining curled up on his side. Three signal bars out of four, were portrayed in the upper left corner. Bert instantly felt a small sense of relief. Sitting up, his stubby fingers fumbled around as he punched in, nine-one-one, on the key pad. After pressing send, on the second ring, a woman's voice answered.

*"Nine-one-one, what's your emergency?"*

"We need an ambulance off of Tyler Road. There's been a horrible car accident," Bert stated as calmly, and coherent as possible.

*"What is your name sir?"*

"My name is Bert. The car has spun off, and hit a tree. My friend is dead. We had to leave the vehicle behind to find shelter from the cold. All they have to do is follow the tracks towards an old farmhouse through the woods and across a field. My other friend needs assistance. She is injured with a head wound," Bert paused. The phone seemed too quiet for comfort. "Hello? Are you still there?" Glaring at the screen, the screen was dark, and the battery was drained "Dammit!" In a fit of anger he chucked the phone with full force, breaking it against a tree.

Bert's only options, were to wait and hope the operator heard enough information to locate him, or try to march to the road. He felt useless.

Trying to piece together tonight's events consumed his thoughts. The more he tried, the further apart the timeline of events seemed to be. Flurries of emotion plagued him.

A glint reflecting off a glass window, caught his attention. Now that the farmhouse provided a blazing light, he could view a rickety tool shed near the home. It was a small structure, maybe eight by ten feet around the perimeter. Cracked red paint peeled off the siding, exposing the gray wood grains beneath. Young trees surrounded the shed, covering the roof in branches.

Bert feebly stood again, lifting himself with the cane. Marching over to the entrance, he entered. Skreeet! A rat scurried between his legs, escaping away from him, and exiting the door. Rusted hammers, screwdrivers, hand saws, and other abandoned tools, hung against the shelved walls. Some tools were dropped on the floor, or resting on a workbench. Hanging upon a curved hook, on the end wall, was a long length of rope. Bert guesstimated the rope was half an inch thick. Rolled up, sagging down into an oval shape, he grabbed it. As he was doing so, he caught another glimpse of something resting above him. Placed on top of the horizontal ceiling rafters, was a toboggan, stretched across the length of the structure.

Bert gingerly climbed on top of the workbench. He almost slipped, but caught himself, by grasping onto an exposed two by four stud on the wall. Reaching up with his right arm, he rotating the sled around ceiling rafters, spaced nearly two feet apart. One end of the toboggan came crashing down to the floor, and the other thunked to the surface of the bench. Descending the workbench safely, he fit his head through the rope loop, to carry it on his shoulders. Picking up the sled, he drug it outside the shed entrance. Studying the wooden toboggan, he was relieved that it was structurally intact. The grain was fading to gray. Varnish was cracked minimally, peeling off in sections. But it wasn't deteriorated enough to diminish its usage.

Leaving it behind, he entered the shed again to scavenge more supplies. He found a dirty canvas tarp, folded, with sections of green mold spreading around the creases. Locating a pocket knife, with a white handle, he unfolded it to reveal a sharp blade. Exiting, he placed all the supplies he found onto the toboggan, and pulled it by a tattered rope, that was previously connected to the vehicle.

Spreading the tarp, on the surface of the toboggan, and ground, he pulled Mary's unconscious body onto it. Wrapping the canvas around her, he used a long length of rope to secure the tarp around her torso, knees, and ankles. Sawing the rope with a pocket knife, he used the remaining length to tunnel under her bindings. Bert constructed a double fisherman's knot, strapping her down near the apex of the sled. Now, Mary was wrapped up by the tarp to remain warm. Also, she was secured enough, to make the journey back to the road.

Small puffs of steam could still be viewed rising from Mary's mouth. Bert had a sense of relief every time her chest rose, and exhaled. He felt confident in her stability.

Using the tattered rope, as reins previously attached to the toboggan, didn't seem like  a wise idea, because of the dry rot. Bert needed more rope. He searched the shed again. Nothing he could use. Bert wandered around the farmhouse yard, while the blaze continued to dance.

Bert spotted a clothing line, spanning between two trees. Approaching, Bert inspected it closely. The wire line was near a quarter of an inch thick. Sawing with a pocket knife, would take too much time, and exert too much energy. Shuffling back to the shed, Bert was tiring down, breathing became heavy. Ignoring the messages his worn out body was trying to convey, he continued to search anyway. Bert found a pair of heavy duty wire cutters. Clipping the line off the trees, he backtracked over to Mary.

Picking up the candles they dropped in the snow when escaping the farmhouse, he walked over to the flames. Lighting both candles, he used one of them to melt the wax on the base. Placing the candles on the toboggan nose, the melting wax sealed to the vehicle. It wasn't much, but at least it would give off enough illumination, to enable his vision along the path to return.

Placing his cane between Mary's rope bindings, so he could locate it later, Bert limped to the apex of the sled. Looping the wire around to the internal curved nose of the toboggan, he wrapped the ends around his hands so it wouldn't slip. Stretching his arm behind, chest forward, he leaned into his body weight.

Bert began to glide the toboggan through the surface of the snow. Each step, sent throbbing pains up his spine, and pressed against his arthritic knees. Through marching stomps, he let out grunts of exhaustion. The fiery farmhouse gradually moved farther away, as the frigid temperature became lower than he remembered earlier. Following the trail of footprints back across the field, he was determined to save Mary's life, even if he died trying. Flurries began to accelerate their descent from the starry sky. Bert picked up his pace, before the previous tracks get covered by new snowfall, and possibly lose his direction back to the road.

Reaching the tree line of the woods, Bert had no choice but to rest. The immense inflammation he felt in his aging body, was slowing him down. His lungs ached, and burned with every inhalation. But he didn't wish for the young lady to freeze. Without exerting physical exercise, her body temperature was sure to drop to dangerous levels. And if he rested too long, he too might succumb to exposure. This urgency, motivated him with a second feat, of determined strength.

It was eerily quiet, except for the occasional wind through the pines, and the crunch of his boots packing down the ice with every stride. Bert was startled, by the surprising hoot of a snow owl. Perched upon a branch in an oak, the bird focused its large eyes onto Bert. The majestic animal gazed at him, like a familiar acquaintance. Bert nodded to the owl, as a sign of greeting to his fellow animal. Although after nodding, Bert felt quite foolish, 'Why would an owl care for a hello, anyhow?'

Long wailing howls of a pack of wolves, interrupted his thoughts. Bert knew the fearsome canines were lurking nearby. He quickened his pace to a full jog, from senses coursing with fear. Growling huffs, bounced the sound waves off the trees. It was difficult to know where they were located. Should the wolves find them, he wouldn't be able to fight them off successfully. Bert and Mary, were being hunted, by ferocious dogs. There was no doubt in his mind, that their scent, was filling the nostrils of the beasts, with hungry anticipation.

Bert gasped when he witnessed the starving gaze of the wolf directly blocking his path. He halted. If he took a step further, the canine would attack. Gray and white fur, whipped around, shielding the animal from the gusts of icy wind. Glowing eyes pierce the darkness. The wolf was alone, temporarily. Bert could hear barking, from the other members of the wolf pack approaching closer. Growling, sharp fangs revealed themselves. Bert removed the pocket knife, extending the blade.

Bert's ears filled with the thumping beats of his heart, like the snare drums of college marching bands. Fear made his stomach ache, as more wolves arrived, surrounding he and Mary. 'This is it,' he thought to himself. 'There is no escape, death is coming.'

"Okay you damn mongrels," Bert spoke aloud. "If we're going to die, I'm taking a few of you with me!"

The first wolf lunged at him. Instinctively, Bert placed his left forearm upward, as the dog's teeth penetrated. Ripping the grains of his muscle, the wolf pulled. He began ferociously stabbing the beast wherever he could, over and over. Yelping, the dog dropped to his side.

Pow! Ratatattat! Multiple gunshots rang out. Frightened wolves galloped away, kicking up ice from their paws. Even the injured wolf was able to escape, limping away, attempting to escape its inevitable mortal wounds. Blood dripped down Bert's finger tips.

Stepping out from the trees, shadowy figures appeared. Their steps didn't create a sound, floating above the surface. Slowly, their color returned. Covered in blood and mud, full of gunshot wounds, and missing limbs; the platoon of deceased veterans revealed themselves. Miller Jones grinned at Bert. Their mouths were moving, in conversation with one another. But he couldn't hear them, or understand what their message was. Sadly, just as rapidly as they arrived, saving Bert's life, their bodies blackened to shadows once again. Leaving Bert alone, with an injured girl, and more of a distance to trudge through.

Bert's eyes watered, a tear rolled down his cheek, but froze to his goatee. He could still recall their young faces, just like the day he met them in boot camp. Those men, full of desperate hope, that one day, they would come home from the jungle. They wanted to feel the American soil beneath their feet again.

Bert felt immense pressure in his chest. Survivors guilt, constricted his body. He shook as he began to weep further. Putting his hands on his knees, kneeling over the ground, he took a moment to reset. Asking himself, as he had many times, 'Out of all those men, why was I the only survivor in my platoon? The war took away so many good souls. What made me so special? Or was it just plain, dumb luck? I didn't deserve it.'

Wiping his sleeve across his eyes, he sniffed up the gooey liquid drainage, dripping from his nose. Picking up his reins again, he continued to pull Mary through the forest. Twisting and turning through the widest areas of trees, for the toboggan to fit between; he heard Mary let out a cough. She wasn't awake yet, but he was glad to hear any noise she created. This meant, hope was still attainable.

Headlights shone off the barks of trees. The volume of passing cars whipped up ahead. With just twenty, or maybe thirty, more yards to go, he made a final surge, reaching close to ten feet of distance, from the edge of the road. Releasing the wire reins, his shoulders slumped forward. Dipping down into the ditch, then back up again, he attempted to flag down any passing vehicles. His legs couldn't take another step. Bert frantically waved his arms up and down, simulating the flapping wings of a bird. But the automobiles kept speeding by.

His vision became blurry. The sky above him, was spinning. The stars sped up in circular rotation. Bert's senses were failing. Up was down, down was up, right was left, left was right. Like the feeling one can get on a roller coaster, his stomach was queasy. Bert's legs buckled, he plopped into the snow near a ditch. Puking up his Christmas dinner from over exhaustion. Bert's eyelids were too heavy to hold open much longer. Sliding down the descent, he pulled to a crawl, next to Mary. Bert's body quit, on his persistent will to continue. He slept near her, unconscious to the world around him.

# Chapter Seven

Stain yellow ceiling tiles, phased into Bert's sight. Flat pillows rested behind his head, supporting the neck. The back of the bed was angled up to thirty degrees. A tube was sticking from the vein, in the bend of his arm. On a mobile metal hooked pole, an IV bag was nearly depleted.

Shifting his head to the right, he could view the town lights outside the window. It was evening. Every street pole, could be observed from this angle, brightly shined with green, red, and clear bulbs. Wreathes wrapped in bows hung upon the poles. The light switch was turned off, except for the hallway florescent light, beaming into the open door of the hospital room. White slide curtains partially blocked his view of the corridor.

Bert lifted the blanket, to reveal a hospital gown draped over his tired body, with a pattern of multiple navy blue sailboats, speckled all long the white fabric. Fresh gauze bandages were wrapped tightly against his left forearm. Reaching over to the bed controls on the stabilizing bar, he pressed the incline button. Humming, the torso section of the bed lifted him. Bert released the button, at about sixty degrees of incline. Clicking a release handle, pushing down the bar on the left side, he scooted, to attempt to leave.

Gingerly sweeping his legs over to the left side of the bed, he gripped the mattress. His feet dangled below. Reaching back, Bert used the bed controls to lower the bed frame closer to the floor. Bert's toes touched the cold, white and gray linoleum tiles. Sliding off the edge of the mattress, his balance was shaky, but he managed to use the IV pole for stability.

Limping, and shuffling his feet simultaneously, he rolled the IV pole along, slightly ahead of his path. Bert's muscles were tight, and extremely sore. The old man's knees clicked aloud for the first six steps. Reaching the door, he peeked out into the hallway. Just a few yards away, facing right, was the nurse station.

A height of the counter surface, reached slightly below the top of a female nurse's crown. With the sound of a typewriter in front of her, she was smashing away at the keys, possibly writing a medical report. Bert thought it was strange, that an outdated use of a typewriter would be used in the twenty-first century. But something even more queer caught his attention. On top of the counter, was a small Christmas tree, about twenty-four inches in height. Under the tree, two tiny presents were placed, wrapped in brown paper, and twine bows.

Bert remembered seeing Christmas trees, throughout this terrifying night. In different locations throughout the evening, there were presents, subtracting from existence. Six presents were in his den. Then after Hannah disappeared, only five remained. Four cardboard packages, were in the attic when they hid from Esther. Three gifts rested under the dilapidated tree, in the farmhouse ruins.

'Now, two presents under the tree in the hospital? Surely, this cannot just be a coincidence. Could it?' he questioned.

The nurse halted her typing, and stood. She was tall, and slightly overweight. Brown hair was swept back into a bun, hastily dropping to the back of her neck.

"Sir, you should be in bed," the female nurse spoke with a soothing tone.

"There was a young lady with me earlier. Her name is Mary. Is she okay?"

"Are you a family member?"

"No, just a friend."

"Are you sure?" she asked. "She claims otherwise."

"What do you mean? I just met her earlier tonight."

"Perhaps you should get some rest." The nurse approached him, attempting to guide Bert back to his room.

"How long have I been here?"

The nurse gently placed her hand beneath his, and gripped his elbow with the other, to support his wobbly form, and ensure a safe travel back to his bed. "You've been here a few days."

"An entire day came and went?"

"Yes, I'm afraid so."

"Wait, can I still see Mary? I just wanted to make sure she's okay."

"Maybe later, right now you need rest."

"Please, I'll only be a few minutes."

The nurse paused, stared uncomfortably at Bert for a few seconds, which felt like minutes to Bert's perspective. Something didn't seem normal about her. Her gaze turned into a void, like a great white shark's eyes. For a brief moment, he could smell the rot of flesh. The nurse's appearance, transformed into a walking corpse. Skin stretched down her face, and her lips were blistered, with pus rolling down her chin. A left eye popped out of socket, swinging side to side from the optic nerve. Her head quivered. Maggots began crawling from her ears. Bert jumped away from her, turning away to run. She grabbed him by the shoulder.

"Are you okay?" the Nurse asked. Bert averted his gaze, opening the left eyelid, followed by the right, ceasing his escape attempt. "Sir, are you okay?" She reiterated. The nurse appeared to be a living, healthy human being. She glared at him, confused by his erratic actions.

"I, I'm sorry. Guess I saw something in the corner of my eye," Bert lied.

"Oh, I understand that," she replied with a smile.

"So, is it okay if I visit Mary?"

"I don't see why not, but first, let's get you into a wheelchair, for safety reasons of course."

"Thank you."

"Hold onto this hallway railing, while I go get it at the station."

Bert did as she asked. Her white shoes squeaked across the floor. Returning with a wheelchair, she engaged the brakes to allow a safe sitting. Bert climbed into the seat, while lifting his legs, as she pushed the pedals into position for his feet to rest upon. He continued holding his IV pole.

"Don't worry. I'll hold onto that for now," she commanded, yet in a polite and professional tone, releasing the IV pole from his grip.

Rolling along the hallway, he couldn't help but be curious, peeking into every room as they passed by. The beds appeared empty from the corridor. Florescent lights flickered, as they traveled to an elevator.

"How far away is she?"

"Oh not far, just one floor down, the second floor." The nurse pressed the elevator button, and they waited a few moments for the doors to open. They entered. *"Rudolph The Red Nosed Reindeer,"* played over the elevator speakers. "I always loved this song," she commented, breaking the awkward silence.

"I like Christmas songs too. They always make me happy." He then questioned,"What is your name? If you don't mine me asking?"

"My name is Mrs. Tod."

"Toad, as in the amphibian?"

"No, it's spelled tee-oh-dee."

"Like Todd, without the extra dee?"

"Sort of, but it's German. It means something completely different."

"What's your first name?"

"Duh roh gah."

"How is it spelled?"

"Dee arr oh gee e. Droge."

"Is that German too? I like the sound of it."

"Yes."

"You don't speak with a German accent."

"It's just a name I was born with."

"You can call me Bert," he spoke politely. The old man tried to make the conversation as friendly as he could, so as not to arouse suspicion that he didn't trust this hospital. He began to believe he was suffering from insanity, or possibly dementia. All these creatures, and the momentary deteriorating appearance of Nurse Tod, created insecurity about his state of mind. He wished to simply dismiss these horrors, as an active imagination, but it felt too realistic.

Ding! The elevator rang out when they arrived to the second floor. Doors slid open. Gloomy corridors of dim lighting, felt out of place for a hospital wing. Bert felt uneasy, when he passed by each room. Agonizing moans filled the air. Looking into one of the rooms, as they trekked by, a man was on the hospital bed, convulsing as he puked chunks of bile into a shiny metal bucket.

Rolling down the hall, Nurse Tod pushed Bert into a room on the left. Mary slept in a hospital bed, with a gray blanket hiked up to her neckline. Cloth bandages wrapped around her head. Mary's eyes were swollen shut, and her cheeks were blotchy.

"I'll leave you here for few minutes. I'll be back," Nurse Tod confirmed, closing the door behind her.

The enclosure was brighter than the other rooms he witnessed in this wing. Bert pushed up the foot pedals of the wheelchair, locked the brakes, and cautiously stood up. "Mary?"

She didn't answer. Her chest motioned up, and down, with deep slumbering breaths. Bert dared not to wake her, although every instinct screamed in his brain to do so.

Walking to the foot of her bed, he glanced back at the glass rectangle built inside the door. They were still alone, Nurse Tod wasn't in the hallway. His curiosity couldn't be held back any longer. Bert wondered what Mary's last name was. Picking up the chart, he read the top of the paper. Mary Simmons was listed as the official name. His suspicions were correct.

The manner in which Simmons, and Olivia spoke, at the farmhouse, hinted that they were all related. The framed photo that was discovered, revealing the couple, couldn't be ignored. Bert recalled the Christmas dinner, Mary was consoling Olivia as tears rolled down her face, like a loving daughter would. "Simmons" wasn't the first name of his butler. It was his last.

But the real question remained. Was this over? How could he explain Hannah, Al, Esther, and Richey's strange deaths? What were those creatures he encountered? Junior?

'Junior!' he remembered. "Junior is Simmons, which means, Al and Esther were his parents," Bert whispered to himself.

"Dad, are you here?" Mary woke, asking in the vocal tone of a frightened child.

"No, I'm sorry Mary. It's just me, Bert," he said, stepping closer to her.

The heart monitor sped up. "I can't see Bert. Where is my Dad?"

"It's okay Mary. Relax. Your head is swollen from the explosion. Once the swelling goes down, you'll see again. Tell me your Dad's name, maybe I can locate him?"

"But you know his name, don't you?"

"Albert Simmons Junior," Bert confirmed, already knowing this knowledge.

"I need my Daddy. He has to save my child."

"Your child? Mary, you don't have a child, do you?"

"They took him away Bert. The doctors, they took him away!"

"Mary, you weren't pregnant a few days ago. You're not making any sense."

"I tried to tell them. I've been clean for months," Mary began to weep.

"I don't understand."

"They think I'm still shooting up. I'm not! Tell them Bert. Tell them I'm clean. Don't let them take the baby."

"Mary, I think your brain is still swollen, honey. You don't have a child."

"Yes I do! I just delivered him! He's here! We gotta get my baby back."

The chart was still in his hand. Bert scanned the page. Traces of heroin were found in Mary's system. A cesarean was administered, to remove the premature, and drug addicted baby.

Disappointed in her, Bert said, "Please tell me you didn't do this Mary. You're a good girl. This isn't like you."

"I'm not good Bert. I'm far from it," Mary revealed, as her lip trembled with regret.

Knock! Knock! Knock! The hospital door opened. Nurse Tod entered. Carrying a spoon in he hand, she began lighting the bottom with Mary's pink lighter.

"What the hell are you doing?!" Bert exclaimed.

"It's time for your medicine Mary. You'll feel so much better."

"Get that shit away from her!"

"Why do you care Bert? It isn't like she's your daughter. You disowned her, remember? Kicked her out of your house. Didn't speak to her for over a decade." Droge Tod stated. Her fingers extended out on her right hand. Tod's fingernails lengthened into syringe needles, soaking up the drugs from the spoon.

By then, Bert was able to strike Tod in the face with a right hook. The nurse wiped the blood from her lip, and grinned. She backhanded him with her left hand, sending him crashing against a wall. He couldn't get to his feet in time. By then, Nurse Tod was hovering over Mary. She stabbed her needle-like talons into Mary's heart.

Her heart monitor slowed down. Beep! Beep! Beeeeeeeeeeeeeeep. Mary's chest didn't rise. Her life ended prematurely. Bert cried out! Picking up a chair, he somehow hurled it with enough strength at Nurse Tod. The legs of the chair struck her in the forehead.

"Scrraaaawwwkkk!" Nurse Tod let out an unearthly, elevated raspy scream. The deteriorated form that Bert witnessed earlier, revealed itself again. "You can't hurt me Bert. I am everywhere. In every family, in every state, and in every country, no one can stop me. My victims seek me out in their darkest times. And I make them feel good. Like floating on a cloud. But I required their worship in return. Their lives are mine now. Very few can resist my temptations, once they've had a taste of the pleasure I give. But they always want more. Behold! My followers are here."

The corridors were flooded with rotting zombie-like corpses. Some of them, still had needles hanging from their arms. Men, women, children, young, or old, it didn't matter. Addiction ruined them, turning them into grotesque creatures.

"Where is Mary's child?"

"Another of my subjects. Of course, he didn't have any choice did he? Even now, he craves the poison pumping in his veins. A last minute gift from his mother. I doubt he'll be able to resist me for long. His soul belongs to me now."

"Please," Bert began to beg. "Let me save the child. Give me a chance."

"Why should I? You couldn't even save your own daughter, your wife, or your sister. In fact, they're dead because of you. Isn't that right, Simmons?"

"What? No! I'm not Simmons!"

Droge Tod laughed maniacally at his ignorance. "Oh, but aren't you? Albert Simmons, Junior!"

"No!" Bert looked down, and ripped out his IV tube and needle. When he lifted his head, the room was empty. The heroin zombies, Nurse Tod, and Mary, were all gone. The wallpaper was ripped down. Mounds of dirt and trash covered the floor. The window, cast pink and orange hues of the sun outside. His shadow covered the floor from the light of a rising dawn.

Wearing the Santa outfit again, he reached down and picked up his cane. Leaving footprints in the dust, he exited the room. Wires and fiberglass ductwork, hung from the ceiling. Piles of fallen ceiling tiles were scattered across the floors. He found a map of the hospital, framed in cracked plexiglass, screwed to a hallway wall. Making his way to the stairs, he slowly descended to the first floor. Echoes of his footsteps bounced off the neglected structure.

Opening the entrance, Bert traveled to a corridor marked, “Nursery.” In the middle of the dilapidated room, he felt a sigh a relief. A newborn baby moved his tiny limbs. Tubes assisted the child’s breathing. Next to the incubation chamber, a chart read the name, “Xavier A. Simmons.” A plastic Christmas tree, with broken stringed lights, was toppled over in the corner of the room. Next to it, was the last gift under the tree.

Fog emanating smoke, rolled in from under the doorways, and broken interior windows. Bert remained calm, as the fog engulfed the area. Accepting the truth, of who he was, he knew the next course of action was crucial. Bert had to confront the monster, of his past. He had to face himself.

# Chapter Eight

Bert stood on the front porch of his home. The entrance door gleamed with a blinding light, spreading from the spaces between the frame. Reaching for the brass handle, he inhaled deeply, and turned the knob. Pushing the door ajar, he stepped inside. Everything was blank, illuminated so brightly, that it irritated his eyes. Gradually dimming, he was transported to the barn, in which he used to play in as a child.

***

Putrid scents of cow manure filled his lungs. The stalls looked taller than Bert remembered. Rough wooden beams, and rafters, filled the ceiling above. A lofted area bridged across the middle. Sunlight beamed into the large open doors, striking the ground ahead. Bert lifted his hands, to the front of his sight line. Small digits and hands, were present. He was a young boy again.

"Junior!" Al called out.

"Yes Papa!" Bert responded.

"You're supposed to be helping me spread out this straw, boy. Can't have your sister doing the chores while you play, now can we? Get over here, and get to work."

"Okay Papa. I'm sorry."

Sprinting over to his father, his height reached the top of Al's waist, hugging him from the side. Gazing upward towards his father, he always seemed strong, impenetrable to weakness. Releasing him, he said, "Okay, okay, I love you too kiddo." Handing a pitchfork over to him, Bert gripped the handle. "That doesn't let you off the hook either," Al laughed.

"Al! Telephone call for you!" Esther shouted from the steps of the farmhouse.

"On my way!" Al exclaimed. Looking down to Bert, Al's face was shrouded because of the sunlight peaking behind him. "Alright Junior, go ahead and start putting straw in the stalls. I'll be back to help you."

"Okay Papa."

Al exited the barn through the open doors, disappearing from sight. Bert rested the pitchfork, onto a structural wood post, reaching up to the ceiling. His sister, Hannah began jumping in the large pile of straw. She wore denim overalls, with a brown and green plaid button shirt. Her red hair appeared orange in the sunlight rays.

Bert challenged her, "Bet you can't flip off the loft and land onto the straw heap."

"Of course I can," she insisted.

"Nope, girls can't do what boys can. They're weaker than men."

"Are not! Let's do it then. I'll show ya."

The children climbed up the ladder to the loft. The pile of straw sat directly below. "I'll go first. Watch this!"

Bert stood near the ledge, bent over, and dropped below, flipping onto his back as he landed safely onto the straw pile. He giggled, as he slid himself to the ground.

Hannah defiantly challenged him, "You just fell. You didn't jump."

"So! I still flipped."

"Nah, I'll do better. I'll jump up, and flip off the ledge. And I bet I'll land on my feet on the straw."

"No way!" Bert dismissed her claim, looking up at her on the loft.

"You don't believe me?"

"Nope, you're just a smelly girl with cooties. You should just play with your dolls."

"I can do it."

"Well, go ahead then! Jump Hannah! Jump!"

*Bert's memory flooded forward the night of the Christmas dinner. When the elderly Bert left the kitchen with Richey, entering the dining room, because of Hannah's scream. Al was consoling his daughter. He remembered Hannah saying, "Daddy, please, I'm not making it up. I saw it. It looked at me! It told me to jump!"*

"Go ahead Hannah! Jump!" The young boy dared her.

Hannah walked backwards, to get an optimal running distance. As she ran, she tripped on a loose board. Trying to catch herself, she clumsily fell off target. Barely missing the straw, she stumbled head first, onto the ground below. Her fragile neck, snapped backward.

***

*Bert was transported to the day of Hannah's funeral. A short wooden coffin was placed in front of the church. A lanky preacher was giving a eulogy.*

Bert stared at the floor. Afraid to look up at Hannah's tiny face in the casket, so angelic in eternal sleep. He could barely see anything through the tears, blocking his vision. Al's arm was wrapped up around the boy. His head rested against his father's chest. Sitting up straight, he gazed over to his mother, Esther. Wearing a black veil over her face, with an ice cold stare.

Turning her attention to Bert, she mouth the words, with a vengeful look in her eyes, "It's your fault."

***

*Bert was whisked away to a hospital waiting room. A doctor walked in, as Esther stood in nervous anticipation of what news he may bring.*

"Is my husband okay? When can I see him?" she asked. Esther's eyes were bloodshot from weeping, and inebriation.

This time, Bert looked up, slightly taller, just a year older. He didn't stand. Bert simply focused at the doctor's expression, as he tried to explain what happened to Al.

"Ma'am, I'm so sorry. We did everything we could. He had a heart attack, known as the widow-maker infarction. An occlusion of his left coronary artery," he paused, realizing she didn't care about the medical explanation. "I am sorry for your loss, Ma'am."

Esther fell to her knees, convulsing from terrible sadness, and mourning her husband. Young Bert refused to believe what he heard. He couldn't fathom the thought of his father passing away. Racing to the double doors, he pushed them open to search for Al.

"Stop! That is off limits!" A nurse called out as he ran past her.

Sprinting from room to room, he found a body in the fifth. The body was covered in a white sheet, with the face shrouded. Bert pulled the cotton sheet away, revealing his father. He shook Al on the arm.

"Daddy! Daddy! Wake up! Wake up! You can't leave me Daddy! I need you! Don't leave me with Mom! Please!" Bert pounded his fists against Al's lifeless corpse. Wailing, the boy reluctantly admitted defeat. He climbed up onto the bed, hugging his father one last time, refusing to let go. "I love you Daddy," he whispered, then sniffled up mucus from his nose. "I always will."

***

*Transforming into an old man, living in the present tense, Bert was leaning against his cane. Inside his foyer, Simmons approached from the Den. His true facial features finally revealed itself as Bert's younger adult image.*

"You were trying torture me, weren't you Simmons?"

"We killed her Bert. We killed Hannah. By doing that, we murdered our father's will to live. It's all our fault."

***

*Bert aged backward to a thirteen year old boy. Richey sat at the kitchen table, across from Bert. It was the same kitchen as the Christmas dinner events, except smaller in size, long before Bert's add-on construction at a later time.*

"Junior, listen, I know your mother has a problem. But she'll get help. I promise. Don't go to the authorities. They'll only put you in an orphanage."

"No!" Bert slammed his fist down onto the table. "I'm tired of her! She doesn't want me here Richey. She's a shitty person."

Richey stood up in a hurry, scolding Bert, "Don't talk that way about your mother! She has an addiction Junior! Esther can't help herself." Richey lowered his voice. "Let's not wake her. Look, in the morning I'll make sure every scrap of alcohol is out of the house. I'll make sure she sees a psychiatrist."

"It won't help. Look at what she does to me," Bert pulled back his sleeve. Burn marks, from cigarettes, with scabs reached up to his bicep. Lifting his shirt, Richey could see the purple imprints of a belt buckle stretched across his abdomen."

Richey's expression changed. He gasped, putting his hand up to cover his mouth. Richey replied, "Oh God, I swear Junior, I didn't know."

"Of course you wouldn't know Richey. You work too much to notice anything. You're supposed to be my step dad. You're supposed to protect me."

"Junior, I truly am sorry," he said, walking over to Bert. Embracing him with a hug, Richey's eyes began to well up. Bert pushed him away. "Your father was my best friend. I swore I would look after you. It won't happen again. I'm getting you out of here. I'll send you to my parents for a while. They're good people. I'll make sure your mother never drinks a drop of alcohol again. In the meantime, she'll get help. When she's better, I'll bring you back."

Bert responded, "What if I don't want to come back Richey? She won't get better. She's just an insect. A goddamn scorpion, ready to stab at me with her poisonous tail."

"Listen, I love you like a son. If she doesn't stop, I'll make sure we both leave, together."

"You, you mean it?" Bert asked with a sliver of hope.

"Yes, of course."

***

"She did get better Simmons. Why should we relive this past?"

"But the damage was done wasn't it Bert? Our mother tried so hard to make us forgive her. But she doesn't deserve forgiveness. We never let her heal. Instead, she died knowing we hated her."

"No, we did forgive her. But that doesn't mean we should forget Simmons. Things got better, even after she died. Richey became more than a stepfather, he became our friend. It's not our fault he died in a car accident."

"But we betrayed him Bert. After all we went through, we ended up being an alcoholic too. Just like our dear mother. We were lower than dirt. Sleeping in our own vomit, and waking up with sluts that gave us the clap? Vietnam was the best thing that could have happened to us. The draft sobered us. Our true nature could be released! It felt good to kill didn't it Bert? You know you liked it. Quite insane we were. Remember that specific sound it makes, when a bullet enters a man's chest? We killed many, didn't we Bert?"

"I see their faces in my dreams, Simmons. I'm not that man anymore. Times were different then. We were soldiers. It was war. You know this. We were drafted for god sakes."

*"We'll take the boy," the shadows whispered.*

"It should have been us, Bert. Dead in that field. Our sins demanded death."

"But Olivia waited for us to get back. We were going to start a family, a life. We survived."

"And how did that turn out?"

"Stop it Simmons. I tried to help Olivia. So did Mary. But there wasn't any way to bring her out of her melancholy."

"Amazing how you can just wash your hands of this Bert. Your mind never left that jungle, while she was alive. Every time she asked for help, you rejected her. Constantly reminding her how selfish she was, never listening to her fears. You know how Olivia's father used to beat her, and torment her when she was a child. It was worse than what our mother did to us. She just wanted to be heard, Bert. All she needed was love, understanding, and attention. But you were trapped in your own memories of war."

"Don't make me relive this! Please!"

***

Little Mary Simmons played in a sandbox in front of the farmhouse home. Scooping up sand, and pouring it over a metal toy van. "Avalanche!" she cried out.

Bert arrived home from work, when he saw his daughter playing. He was dressed in a blue suit, with a whiskey spot dropped on his red tie. "Whatcha doin' Mary?" he asked, while taking a swig from a flask.

"Daddy, it's a sand avalanche. Oh no! The van is broken down, Daddy."

Bert kissed her on the top of the head. "Where's your Mother? I have some good news for her."

"She's taking a bath Daddy. She's been there all day. I'm hungry. I haven't eaten since breakfast."

"I'll make sure dinner will be done soon okay. Let me check on Mommy, and I'll be back."

Opening the front door, he stepped inside the same home he lives in presently. Traveling up the stairs to the master bedroom, he heard a "slush" beneath his feet. Water had soaked the carpet. Entering, he trudged across the floor. "What the hell? Olivia, do we have a leaky pipe?"

*Simmons' tongue whipped up her left forearm, slicing a vertical wound. Then descending the razored tongue down her right forearm.*

Turning the knob to the bathroom door, he crossed the threshold. Olivia naked body was floating in the bathtub. Her arms rested over the ledge of the tub. Long bloody slits were sliced vertically up both wrists. Crimson colored bathwater surrounded her body, while the faucet continued to spew water.

***

Bert wailed, while Simmons smiled. "Why did you show me this again? To punish me? I didn't kill her."

"But your words pushed her to suicide. Don't you deserve it Bert? Don't you deserve punishment?"

"I tried so hard to help Olivia. I raised my daughter the best I could."

"But Mary died alone Bert! She ran away off to Germany when you disowned her. She suffered alone, in a hospital bed, vomiting herself to death from withdrawal, perishing, during Xavier's delivery. You had the money to continue her rehabilitation. Why didn't you keep trying?"

"I didn't know what to do Simmons! I tried everything else. She went to rehab so many times I lost count! There's no instructions on this sort of thing."

"Doesn't matter Bert. You gave up on her. What are you doing?" Simmons stepped back as Bert approached his former self.

"I can't change the past Simmons. But I can do one thing."

"Get! Get away from me!" Simmons exclaimed.

"I will forgive you. I will forgive me. I will forgive, us." Bert gripped onto Simmons, squeezing his arms around him.

Embracing the pain of his former self, Simmons struggled. But eventually, succumbed to Bert's love. Simmons' body created a glow, merging with Bert's frail elderly body.

Bert dropped to his knees, inside the den of his home. Placing his hands on the carpet rug, he glanced up, towards his brightly lit Christmas tree. Under the tree, was a solitary present. It faded away, and was left empty.

***

Bert woke up on the couch. Gripping onto his cane, pulling himself up, he stood. He felt a sense of relief, for the first time in years. But he also felt a yearning, to see his grandson for Christmas. He raised the boy after Mary died long ago. Xavier was like his own son, even though, Mary could never be replaced in his heart.

Strolling over to the house phone, he passed by a calendar page, with an "x" marking off the date of December 21st."Carol of the Bells" pushed out its melody through the speakers in the ceiling. Picking up the cordless receiver, he traveled to his favorite chair located in the study. He took a moment to watch the flames dance inside the fireplace. Dialing a number, he placed the receiver up to his ear.

On the third ring, a man's voice answered, "Hello?"

"Xavier?"

"Pop, good to hear from you. How are you?"

"Oh, I'm fine. Listen, I know you said you wouldn't be able to make it for Christmas this year, but I was hoping I could try to convince you one last time."

"Oh Pop, I wish I could, but I'll be working on Christmas Eve. I'll be off a few days after Christmas morning though. Why don't you come to New York? I can get you a plane ticket. Stephanie and I would be happy to have you visit for the holiday. But I understand if you're in too much pain. This cold weather is dreadful to you."

"No need to buy the ticket, son. I'll be there."

# Chapter Nine

Bert sat on the backseat of a New York City taxi cab. Riding through Manhattan, he enjoyed staring outside the window, looking up at the skyscrapers moving past him. Pulling into an underground garage of a red bricked apartment building, the concrete pylons held the structure to street level. The taxi cab came to a complete stop near the elevator.

"That'll be, twenty-two dollars," the female driver informed Bert.

He handed the driver a pair of twenty dollar bills. "Keep the change."

Closing the yellow door, he waved to the driver, as she drove away. He scanned the underground parking lot, lit up with florescent lights down the sections. Nearly thirty feet away, the bulbs flickered. Between the pulsing lights, a quick moment of the Widow Maker's presence revealed itself. When one of the florescent tubes shattered, the Widow Maker dispersed, just as rapidly as he appeared.

Bert gulped, but tried to calm himself. He remembered the words of the Widow Maker when it said, "Slowly beating my song, your body is weak. I will see you again, but it is not you I seek."

After his night of terror, Bert thought it was all a dream. But he couldn't help but wonder if the Widow Maker stalked him, like it did to his father. He hoped to see his grandson, at least one last time, before the terrible creature returned. Taking in deep fluttering breaths, he became emotional. His eyes glassed over. Bert questioned, "Is this my last Christmas?" Pressing the elevator button, the doors separated. Bert stepped inside. His index finger trembled, as he pressed the lit button, to the ninth floor. Bert unzipped his black coat, with a faux furred hood, revealing a festive sweater underneath. The background of the wool sweater was navy blue, with snowflakes descending around Santa, and his flying reindeer. Blinking stars covered the night sky of the sweater, when he pressed a hidden button on his left breast. The twinkly lights, steered his mood to a joyous frame of mind. "After all, it was only a dream. Right?" Bert spoke aloud.

Ding! Stepping out the elevator, he dragged his feet down the white walled corridor. Reaching the apartment number, nine-zero-three, bolted to a plaque next to the reddish stained door, his anxiety diminished away. Bert pressed the door bell. He could hear a muffled conversation through the door, getting louder upon approach.

"You gonna get that?" Xavier asked.

"Just a minute!" Stephanie's voice called out.

"It's probably Pop. Tell him to come in, my hands are inside cookie dough right now."

A petite Vietnamese female opened the door. Her long dark hair was tied back into a ponytail. A streak of purple hair color, brightened up her features. Wearing a red and green checkered sweater, with a picture of a snowman imprinted on the front, and blue denim pants, she greeted Bert."

"Papa Simmons!" The woman warmly hugged him. Releasing him, hands gently squeezing the old man's shoulders, she replied, "How are you? I would have met you downstairs in the elevator if I had known you'd arrived."

"No need Stephanie, I am perfectly capable of making it up here by myself."

"Well, you look great. I love your ugly sweater too. I know it's silly, but we figured we'd try it out this year."

Bert joked. "Oh, I love your's too. Looks like something a Kindergartner would pick out."

Laughing together, Stephanie pressed her right hand to Bert's upper back. "Xavier is making cookies. Come on in."

Stephanie allowed Bert to enter first, then strolled past him. The apartment was modern. Glass encircled most of the living room, giving a beautiful view of the lights of the big city. White curtains were open, tied back in a sash on the edges of the windows. A chocolate brown, leather sofa and love seat, centered the room. A flat screen television, hung upon the only wall space in the living room. Festive holiday lights, of multi colors, reflected off of the glass near the Christmas tree. Gifts wrapped in brown paper, and twine bows, were placed below the tree. Stephanie noticed Bert's admiration of the presents.

"I see my boy has kept the tradition," Bert smiled with pride.

"Yeah, Xavier told me never to have any other wrapping paper for the gifts. He said it reminds him of you."

"I'm honored."

A man with caramel colored skin, and short dark hair, approached from the open space of the kitchen. Xavier's facial expressions reminded him of Mary. He was wearing a green sweater, with an enormous holly wreath stitched into the front. "Pop," Xavier grinned. "You're just in time," he proclaimed holding out his arms and hugging his grandfather.

"So, how is the best chef in all of New York doing?" Bert questioned with a sense of admiration for his grandson's accomplishment.

"Doing great Pop, helping the world get fat, one dinner at a time," Xavier giggled.

***

After an untraditional Christmas dinner, of caesar salad, filet mignon, roasted asparagus, lobster tails, and red skinned garlic mashed potatoes; Bert rested his tired bones on the couch. Xavier poured raspberry white chocolate creamer into the coffee, and brought out freshly baked gingerbread cookies to Bert and Stephanie. She carried on a conversations about her music career, and Xavier's restaurant.

Xavier and Bert, sung along to the chorus, as Stephanie strummed "Rockin' Around The Christmas Tree," on her Fender acoustic guitar. She played a few more songs, while Bert tapped his legs to the beat. Afterward, they settled down to stream a movie.

"Why do you guys watch Scrooged, instead of a classic Charles Dickens version?" Stephanie asked.

"Because Bill Murray, is awesome," Xavier confirmed. "Enough said."

"Can't argue that one," Stephanie agreed.

"There is so much pain in the world," Bert chimed in. "Comedy is the best medicine to get through it."

Stephanie smiled, and raised her second cup of decaffeinated coffee. Xavier and Bert followed her example. "Merry Christmas," she announced. They clinked their coffee cups together, and took another sip.

***

Exchanging gifts at eight o'clock on Christmas Day, was a bit unusual for most households. But Xavier insisted upon waiting for his grandfather to arrive to New York, before opening the gifts.

"Here Pop, I got this for you."

"You didn't need to get me anything. I already have everything I want."

"I know, but it's just a simple gift."

Xavier handed him a red envelope, decorated with candy cane designs. Bert opened the flap, and pulled out a card. Inside was a photograph of a sonogram. He beamed with excitement.

"Is this? Is this what I think it is?" Bert asked.

"He or she is your new great grandchild. We're expecting in June. We waited a few months before we told you. The plan was to tell you on New Years, you know, to celebrate new beginnings. But Xavier was too impatient, he couldn't keep it in much longer," Stephanie laughed.

Joy filled Bert's eyes and smile. "This is the best news I could ever hope for. Any names picked out yet?"

"Well, if it's a girl, we're thinking of naming her Alberta. But if it's a boy, we're going to name him after me," Xavier answered.

"I am very happy, for the both of you. And I am very honored you would consider naming her after me. If she's a girl of course." Bert sincerely stated.

"Well, Pop, you raised me by yourself. You deserve it. And what's great is that we'll be sure to visit more often. Now that I hired another manager to run the restaurant, I'll need more time to spend with the family."

"Thank you. I will keep her picture with me all the time. I look forward to meeting our new family member."

***

Later in the evening, Bert stood up to leave. "Well, I guess I should call a cab to go back to the hotel."

"You can still stay here if you want, Pop." Xavier offered.

"No, it's fine. Besides, I already paid for the next few nights. Do you mind walking me to the elevator, Xavier?"

"Of course Pop."

Stephanie hugged Bert, but stayed behind while Xavier accompanied him out the entrance door, into the corridor. Xavier noticed Bert walking even slower than he normally does. "Are you okay? You seem tired Pop. Sure you don't want to stay. I can run to your hotel, and pick up your suitcase."

"No, no thank you." Bert halted, gazing towards the elevator door. He turned to Xavier and spoke, "I am proud of you. My greatest accomplishment in life was raising you, my son. Whatever happens to me, please take care of yourself, and your new family. And always treasure Stephanie and that baby."

"Pop, you're scaring me. What's wrong?"

"Please, it's best if I go now."

"I will do no such thing. Tell me what's wrong."

"I'll…..I"ll tell you tomorrow. Please, I need you to go back. Spend the rest of your Christmas with Stephanie. Start your own traditions."

"Pop, please you're really not acting right. Tell me."

"I'll see you tomorrow. I'm just tired, that's all son," Bert smiled.

"Okay Pop," Xavier gave in. "I'll see you tomorrow, right?"

Bert nodded. Then he became distracted. "Stay away from him." Bert took a stance in front of Xavier.

The Widow Maker stood just a few yards from him. "He is not destined, to perish by my hand. The one I need, is you, old man."

Vines crept up the hallway, blocking the elevator. "Mister Bones is here. I'm going to see Dad, and Hannah soon. I am almost ready," Bert courageously accepted his fate.

"Pop what are you talking about? Ready for what?" Xavier asked. He couldn't see the Widow Maker, or the vines. It was only visible to Bert.

"Wait, can you give me just a minute? I have one more thing to say to my grandson," Bert requested to the Widow Maker. "Please." The Widow Maker nodded, allowing him a final request. Turning around to Xavier he spoke, "Don't let my passing ruin your Christmases to come. It should always be a joyous time. I have lived a long life Xavier. Its had ups and downs, but it was a good life. This has been the best Christmas, I have ever had."

"Pop, I'm calling an ambulance. You're not going anywhere. You have a lot of good years left. We'll get you to a hospital."

Bert pulled the sonogram picture of his new grandchild, from his breast pocket, stared at it one last time. "She is precious."

"Pop, I insist you must come back to the apartment with me right now."

The Widow Maker thrust its long fingers around Bert's torso. Bert dropped to his knees in front of Xavier. But the only thing he could view, was the man who raised him, suffering from a massive heart attack. Xavier held onto his grandfather yelling, "Call nine-one-one! Call nine-one-one!"

Mister bones stood over Bert, with his right hand held out. "Come with me Bert. Your time is up. Hannah is waiting to play. Your father misses you."

Bert reached out, and his heart stopped pumping. His arm dropped, his body fell limp, resting in Xavier's arms. Bert stared off, with a peaceful expression on his face. A grateful smile, was his last muscle movement. It was Bert's last Christmas.

# Chapter Ten

Two members of the United States Army folded, and presented the American Flag to Xavier, at the gravesite. A bugler proceeded to play Taps. Xavier's eyes were red, irritated, and swollen from mourning the loss, of the only father he ever knew. Stephanie held his shaking hands. A mahogany wood coffin, shined with varnish, rested above a six foot hole, to be lowered after the family, and friends, take their leave.

Many of the townsfolk approached Xavier and Stephanie on that day. Everyone in attendance wore Santa hats, in honor of his love of Christmas. It was bitterly cold, the snow had compacted to ice. It was a short service because of the weather.

Stephanie and Xavier visited the graves of Olivia, and Mary, resting beside Bert. He began placing single, long stem red roses on each of their tombstones. He felt the cold stone atop Mary's grave, and traced out the letters of her name with his gloved finger. He was robbed of the chance to speak to her. Yet, he remembered all the good stories Bert used to recite about his mother. In a sense, it was almost like he knew her well enough to miss her.

A reception was provided at Bert's estate. Xavier kept the home decorated with the Christmas decorations Bert left behind. His grandfather loved the winter holidays, and he honored his memory further, by keeping the lights bright, and cheery. Holiday music played softly over the speakers. Mrs. Purse, and Claude, prepared the meals, one last time, for their deceased employer. Some people ate their fill. Others, became inebriated from egg nog.

Xavier tapped his glass and announced, "Attention! Attention everyone!" The guests stopped what they were engaged in, and gave him their focus. "First of all, I want to say, thank you to all who attended Pop's funeral. Secondly, I want to let you know, that my grandfather's estate, will have a new purpose after today. Stephanie and I, thought it would be wise to transform this property, to a cause my grandfather believed in. Since we don't need to keep this particular property, and we don't need his money, we chose to give back to those suffering. In honor of him, and my mother, this will be a rehabilitation facility for veterans, to overcome any drug or alcohol addictions. We'd rather have them here, getting well, than sleeping out on the streets. Mrs. Purse and Claus will continue to work here, to provide meals for those patients. Professionals will be hired, to treat victims of substance abuse. Pop had enough funds in his account, to hopefully keep it running for at least three years. We are exploring new ways to get financial aid from the government, to keep this place afloat afterwards. This will be known as the Albert Simmons Facility. So please, enjoy yourselves today, because that is what Pop would've wanted. Thank you."

***

It was late August. Xavier watched as hospital beds were being delivered through the front door. The furniture had been sold at auction, to assist in paying for the expenses. Xavier didn't know if, or how long the new rehab center would survive. But even if they had a few good years of helping others, it was worth it in his opinion.

The new staff was cleaning the rooms, preparing inventory, and setting up the filing systems before the grand opening the next day. Xavier took a few days off from work, to oversee things before going back to his normal life. Xavier hired a professional administrator, to keep the rehab facility running smoothly.

Stephanie was breastfeeding their daughter, Alberta Simmons, on a park bench in the front yard of the estate. With the open window, he could hear Stephanie singing to Alberta. Xavier smiled, realizing how good his life truly was. He took Bert's advice, and enjoyed his family.

The place looked different without the furniture inside. Xavier took a walk around. Strolling, room after room, inspecting the new beds, it didn't seem like home anymore. Entering Bert's empty master bedroom, he had an inclination to walk into the attic.

All belongings in the attic were gone. Yet, Xavier didn't want to leave. He couldn't come up with an excuse as to his purpose for visiting the attic. But eventually he started to exit, when he heard two children giggling. Scanning the room, he didn't see anyone. But he caught a glimpse of what appeared to be a small shadow running behind him. But then, it was silent again.

A random word popped in his head, like a whisper in his ear. "Farmhouse" was the word that penetrated his thoughts.

That same afternoon, Xavier drove up the long unkept driveway, to the farmhouse in which Bert grew up in. Small pine trees, and tall grass, made it difficult to drive his truck back to the property. The house was burned down years ago. Only the foundation, a tool shed, and a deteriorating barn remained. Exiting out of his truck, he opened the creaking door of the barn, and entered.

Birds tweeted from the holes in the roof. Cobwebs covered every corner. The straw rotted away a long time ago. He was just about to leave, when he was tapped on his back.

"Excuse me, have you seen my sister," the young boy asked.

"Wha, what are you doing here? This is private property" Xavier stated, shocked by the fact that he thought the place was vacant.

"I live here you silly goose. Have you seen my sister? We're playing hide and seek."

"What's your name?"

"They call me Junior."

"Junior?"

Xavier heard a child's giggle. A little girl darted past them, with red curly hair. Junior took to flight after her. The children faded into thin air as they ran off. Xavier jogged after them, but they were already gone. It dawned on him, who the two children were.

He spoke aloud, "I love you Pop. I always will."

# AVAILABLE NOW!

## THE ELISHA AMULET
## ENIGMAS & EMPIRES: BOOK ONE
### BY BRAD CARR

A portion of mankind has survived a mass extinction event; with the assistance of the enigmatic Messengers. Several centuries later, colonists brave the uncharted territories to set up outposts, and expand their empires. When nature has evolved at an accelerated rate, the land is teaming with hostile predators, and dangerous weather patterns.

The Elisha Amulet is a tale of adventure, horror, love, war, and the complexities of the human condition. How will their actions affect the world? Can human beings create a better Earth? Are they doomed to repeat their destructive behavior?

Made in the USA
Columbia, SC
18 December 2017